Richard Watson Dixon

Christ's company and other poems

Richard Watson Dixon

Christ's company and other poems

ISBN/EAN: 9783337206772

Printed in Europe, USA, Canada, Australia, Japan

Cover: Foto ©Andreas Hilbeck / pixelio.de

More available books at **www.hansebooks.com**

CHRIST'S COMPANY

AND

OTHER POEMS.

CHRIST'S COMPANY

AND

OTHER POEMS.

BY

RICHARD WATSON DIXON, M.A.,

OF PEMBROKE COLLEGE, OXFORD.

LONDON:

SMITH, ELDER AND CO., 65, CORNHILL.

——

M.DCCC.LXI.

TO

HIS FATHER,

JAMES DIXON, D.D.,

𝔗𝔥𝔢𝔰𝔢 𝔓𝔬𝔢𝔪𝔰

ARE DEDICATED BY

THE AUTHOR.

CONTENTS.

Christ's Company.

St. Paul.

PART OF AN EPISTLE FROM GALLIO, THE DEPUTY
OF ACHAIA, TO HIS BROTHER SENECA.

YES; I am grown incapable, 'tis true,
To comprehend our fathers what they were;
But so are all men now, and so are you.
This fallen age can neither see nor hear
The heroic strength of thought which laid
Itself to work, and conquest made
From the wide Infinite displayed
To its wide eyes, and in that trade
Of region conquest carried men by tribes
To people its new colonies: upbraid,
Banter not me, my Stoic, for thy gibes
Be double-edged; I mean that thought
Of Homer or of Plato brought
A tract unknown, perhaps unsought,
To man's domains; and men upcaught,

1

As in a bark, by such thoughts' mightiness,
Were rapt together to the new-found port,
And there got apanage, with no dangerous press
Of numbers, and no famine, for
Such thought was as the harvest store
Of diverse grains for usance, or
Such that each man could bite its core—
Each of a million; yes, that was the age
Of Argonauts; but we who now explore,
We who are writing up the present page
In earth's accounts, can only just
Sharpen a thought which may or must
Touch one soul only to its lust:
No region conquest here, no trust
In each of millions that we speak for him;
Can more than one find room upon the thrust
Point of a pin ? We make a splinter trim.
Yes, and we subdivide at best
The realms of old at large possessed;
This truth stings you like all the rest:
We are not great, it is confessed.

    But there's another danger, solemner ;
The thoughts that work within our children's breast,
Shall we miss these? Our children make demur
To thy sad creed, e'en while we see
The old age rotting utterly,
And we in ruin well agree.
Yes, there is hope of things to be;

Here, while our legionaries from this hill
Look lazily along the languid sea,
Where the white sails wear windward, waving still
With flagging arms to one another:
What bring the galleys as they row there,—
Ind spice, or Cretan grit; or smother
Isle slaves in the monoxylo there?
Yields earth no more to earth's monopolizer
Than such cheap tribute? Nothing rarer, loather,
Than these mean gains? Sad earth! dost thou despise her.
Ostian-mouthed Rome, so much as this?
Dost thou demand no more? Dost miss
No gifts of earth, but tithe anise,
Still murmuring, Let be what is?

   I say, a thought brain-warm and new may grow
In any skull to light up the abyss
Of any nature, till it overflow
(I'll tell you something by and by)
On all the nations, and off-wry
Our business-like supremacy.
For instance, our belief is high;
We are the few for whom the many work:
Suppose it should be bruited in reply,
That nature moves the world in equal cirque;
How wildly should we retograde
Confounded from the web we've made
O'er all the world with spear and spade!
Again, our creed is now our trade,

That the brute multitude may crouch and pray
At popular altars, little reverence paid
By us, who supervise the popular way,
Aristocrats, philosophers:
Suppose an intimation stirs
That God holds by His worshippers,
The swine are right and wisdom errs:
Then, all are right but thou and I and I,
And there is hooting where a fool occurs;
Brother, behold a possibility!
Changes may come; see how the air
Stirs curls that leave the forehead bare   .
Of your Domitian, so aware,
While you by hint and dint prepare
His soul with Stoic maxims for the world,
And with Greek dramas and such other fare
For growing upwards rightly trimmed and curled.
You Stoic poet, is it well
To blow the wrong end of the shell,
Concluding with a Stoic spell
All life as in a citadel,
Half active, and half theoretic; so,
Just as the father of your porch did tell?
     At least you rightly keep your creed, to go
Retracing with poetic skill
The springs Castalian rill by rill!
Those stories anciently did thrill
The blind man of Olympus hill.

Your Hercules I've read, as good almost
As if in Trachis written; still, yet still
An age whose greatest poet is a post
Of that old porch, is a strange age,
   I am no Stoic, yet a sage,
Living in Greece here, where yet rage
Some flutterers 'gainst your iron cage:
We are Platonists in Greece here, we maintain
A various expectation, which bids gauge
The world as not set in this state and strain
For ever; hold in spite of sin
A chastity of mind wherein
Some glimpse of that reserve we win,
Which Essence holds amidst the din
Of outward life and death: since man is base,
Is nature base, doth God fail? Not so thin
Of faith am I; nay, though I grant this phase,
This present, which we all abhor,
May be the last save one that o'er
The world shall pass, yet I ignore
Thy sentence, " There remains no more."
Nay, there's an infinite nothing; we shall come
Thither at least, and have not reached that shore;
We have at least then so much floating room.
   Now with your leave let me rehearse
In brief what prompts me, the reverse
Of your conclusion; why I nurse
This hope of better out of worse.

Five days ago held I a curule hall :
A heap of Jews rushed, mad as if the thyrse
Drave them : they haled along a certain Paul
As prisoner, whom they did accuse
Of those strange questions of the Jews
Of which I gave you lately news :
Their laws, they said, he did refuse
To worship by ; among their heretics
Numbered him ; but what chiefly served to bruise
Their Jew galls was that he had dared to mix
Them with the Gentiles ; he had said
That all men have one common Head,
One common law, one common bread,
Life, death, flesh, spirit, hope, and dread.
These wretched Jews are quite as proud as we ;
Moreover, Paul affirmed one, sometime dead
By Roman law, a seer of Galilee,
To be alive : I think I wrote
Something of this report remote
To illustrate this very thought
That the dead die not ;—time will show 't.
This seer then Paul affirmed to be the Christ,
Or prophet, for whose advent the Jews doat.

All this so angered me, I seized one priest
And scourged him, drove the rest away,
Dismissed their prisoner—hold here—stay—
Their prisoner—what may I say ?
Describe those features ? He did sway

An arm and side towards his slanderers,
And fixed an eye upon me like the ray
Of humid star; a certain reverence errs
From further portrait, but he seemed,
A fire-calm soul; a something dreamed
Between us, as his eyeballs gleamed
With inner vision, which outbeamed
And sunned him, as I had beheld a man
Had gone through all the forms of thought esteemed
Amongst us, by the which we think we can
Gain the truth's truth; I think that he
Had taken from them all the fee,
Nor failed to find not one to be
The knowledge, but had found the key
Some other way, he looked beyond them all,
Yet far from sadness, confident and free,
As if he held them still, let nothing fall
Of all that ever he had learned,
But all by inner force had turned
To one harmonic; I discerned
A pathos which not flamed but burned—
A pathos which consisted in the truth,
As I should call it, not from passion churned,
Not tearful pathos suddenly uncouth,
But rising from the very might,
With which he held the Infinite;
As if some moment past his night
Had changed to glory in a blight

Which withered all desire except to tell
How God did once through all his senses smite.
I am too old to think old things : 'tis well ;
Such men would die, for what they hold ;
He has seen that which doth enfold
His eyesight always, yea, upmould
His nature, which nor heat nor cold
Can suffer in the welding glow of faith.

     I questioned Barrhus why he lowered the gold
Spiral upon my lituus, which he hath,
Until Paul's exit, doing force
To Rome's majesty ; this of course
Insufferable by the laws
Divine and human ;—whence the source
Of such a strange neglect I had observed ?
Barrhus, my oldest of apparitors,
Fixed his grim head towards me, never swerved,
Weeping stone tears from Scythian eyes,
And clipped me such a mint of lies—
Or truths—heart-told in any wise,
About Paul's preaching ;—novelties
I almost thought, until I thought again
You say that nothing new can ever rise ;
He said that Paul was one of many men,
Who words and works and wonders show,
In name of Him their nation slew,
Whom they aver to live anew,
Whom they allege to Greek and Jew,

In whose name they do bid all men repent,
With many other doctrines which ensue
From this; even Barrhus spoke as he were sent
To sound this one word to me then
Straight out from heaven, not as if men
Had taught it him, and he again
Taught me a secondhand refrain.
The sum of all was hope in things to come,
And faith that gives hope substance in our pain,
And love that perfects faith; yes, love the sum
Of sums: the sweetness in the thing
Seemed here, that love was named the ring
Which linketh man to God, the wing
Which strikes the eternal shadowing
With one firm shadow; the great category
(Rest here, rest here) from which the truth doth sing,
Through every other form with brightest glory.

   Winds weary with the old sea tune
Slide inland with some cloud, and soon
From woods that whisper summer noon,
Weigh their wight wings with odour boon;
So I, long salted in our ocean drear
Of disbelief that Essence can be won
By any form of thought invented here,
Felt such a gush of joy about
My heart-roots, as if in and out
'Twas life-blood billowed; and as stout
As once we sent the battle-shout,

Pitching clear notes against barbaric din,—
Oh, brother, my soul's voice against the rout
Of unbeliefs a man doth nurse within,
Arising and protesting wild,
Spake, speaking out untruth defiled ;
Spake, speaking in the truth exiled ;
Spake, Little head and weary child,
Come home, God loves, God loves through sin and shame;
Come home, God loves his world : and thy so-styled
Instincts, which whispered this even in the name
Of doubts and of carnalities,
Were true conclusions, nature-wise ;
In thy old scorned formalities
And creeds, God looks thee in thine eyes !
   Wherefore believe again thine ancient lore,
For whatsoever Reason doth devise,
Her fiery wings and fire-cloud cars to soar,
They truly gain the living height,
Because as their most proper freight
They carry love, the infinite
Of man, up to the rapturous site
Of love, the infinite in nature spread.
Shall forms in nature always play at sleight
With forms in man, that nature's chief and head ?
Nay, God is an authority,
We deem, in nature ; let Him be
Authority in us, that we
Hold this for certainty, that He

Yields up Himself to all our grasps of thought—
Our little nets cast in the shoreless sea,
Our dartles launched in skilled or skilless sort,
Our reason in its many modes,
Its paths lead to the star abodes,
Spherical music lights those roads
To love's true ending, which is God's.
O Love, thou art the secret of our God ;
Thou art, O Love, the centre of heaven's codes ;
The due thou art by all to all things owed !
    This love within me grew alive
So late in this my life, I strive
To give it language; do thou give
Me audience ; we so late arrive
Where we have been so many years agone ;
Yet think of this, with whom should God connive
At such a madman as would gather stone
For his own grave ?   Rather be built
Houses for dwelling with the silt
Of every creed and knowledge, spilt
From the deep waters, which do lilt
With prescient music unto mortal ears,—
Plena sunt omnia Dei ; in our guilt,
Failure and pain this very love inheres.
    I wrote all this to thee last night
Beneath my lonely chamber light,
Impelled through the long hours to write
Up to this point, at which the blight

Of the stealthy morning withered my pale lamp.
And in my vases all the fir-cones lite
Drew their brown mouths a little wider, ramp
Sweet briars with all their berries red,
A palsy took the arbute dead
Asleep till now; he shook and said,
It is high morning overhead,
Where are my birds that sported in my boughs?
The nearer cones no answer breathed, afraid
To lose an instant of their dear carouse
Of the new morning's life divine;
Then first I slept amid the shine
Of all my loving flowers quirine;
And then Paul's face, which did decline
All through the broken waters of my sleep,
Changed wonderfully in a magic sign,
Became in part another's, part did peep
A visage at me terrible,—
'Twas my own look, I knew half well,
My very self; dead mutterings tell
This truth to me; and then the spell
Wrought so that through one ghostly countenance
Two souls did strive to speak, to think, to quell
Each other; then I woke and tell my chance.

Paul spake of One: what man is He,
We ask; what other could He be
Save whom I saw, whom all may see
Of us—another and the Me?

Thou wouldst inquire concerning Him, of whom
Spake Paul—the Christ ?   My dream I tell to thee,
I saw another striving to become
Myself in self; this was the Christ
I think, be sure I have not missed
Paul's meaning, that God's Word uprist
Doth grant the truth to all who list.
Oh, just, and pious, and pitiful heart of God !
There is one Word of Truth who makes acquist
Of human words pronounced in our exode,
From other unto other faith—
Most holy word, as Philo saith
(Another Jew) doth knit the rath
Unto the late with equal breath.
    God grant He may have whispered unto me,
For some fulfilment this poor soul to graith ;
God grant He may have walked in Galilee,
For there belike my love may dwell ;
From this full morning breathes the smell
Of olden years ; from hidden dell
A wind breathes over deserts fell
With whitened bones.   Farewell, farewell.

St. John.

I.

NOTHING has come to the night except the moon :
I see her now; the black and heavy clouds
Rustle in foam before her, tossed and strewn,
    As when at first God's word the clammy crowds,
Half mist, half water, and all ghost, upfroze,   .
    And bared for man the nether firmament
Between the sea and sky, what time the rent

II.

Clouds like a garment parted from it, and close
    The dark fogs sauntered earthwards; now as soon
Yon clouds part upwards, downwards; and outflows
    Vast amber, and the night in happy boon
Is happy now, solemn and clear and cold;
    And full of happy love, broods love—possessed
O'er the dark world, like dove upon her nest.

III.

And I am happy now, so manifold
    The past is, and the present so serene :
Thought I my soul was ready for the gold
    Of visions? but they come not; therefore e'en
As ever, let me think to keep my soul
    Fixed on the whole circumference, which weds
    The centre ever to itself, and spreads

IV.

In light like waves for ever; on the whole
    Of love in love divinely multiplied;
Not generated in the onward roll
    Of ages, though to men 'tis centuried;
But rather in all points of time perfected,
    As in the bosom of the mind divine,
    So in the thoughts of life which thence outshine;

V.

And thirdly, in the sparkles thence deflected
    Into the bosom of this world of man;
In oracles and laws of grace connected
    Through the six ages; God alone, who can
Know how the stream of time doth measure round
    Into a breathing circle held within—
    The eternal circle which doth both begin

VI.

And end it; He alone can know the sound
    Which that glad circle in its rounding makes
In both my ears: for say, was I not found
    In the blest bosom of that love, which slakes
Our human thirst, when all the rest at gaze
    With distant eyes were murmuring, Is it I?
    Lord, is it I?   And think ye no reply

VII.

Did make me nearer to the hidden ways
    Of love, no response beat into my ear
From that deep heart which pulsed the awful rays
    To the eyes beneath whose curve I did upsteer
My reverend gaze, whilst holding solemn state
    In the upper room;—no benediction pressed
    Like a spear's head of bliss into my breast?

VIII.

Yea, truly, as I then beheld elate
    The very form itself of love indeed;
And comprehended in a moment's fate
    That which all comprehending doth exceed,
By science all incomprehensible;
    Incomprehensible things comprehending,
    So ever since that saintly ray's first sending

IX.

The bliss renews itself in visions still,
   And urges me for ever to aspire
To that great knowledge which drew out my will
   To ecstasy, as fire to flame draws fire;
And thus last night the triple period
   Saw I of love; beheld I love in man,
   In angels, and in God; that love began

X.

In agony, lived in service, but in God
   Existed in a wise no tongue may tell;
That, as flowers issue from the underclod,
   Man's anguish gives angelic love its shell
Of service; whence the angels owe to man
   Much bliss; of love and anguish God doth mix
   Peace, which He gives His world in golden pyx.

XI.

I saw last night three boding crows which ran
   Before my feet; I followed, and they sped
Their flight; I followed still each flapping van,
   That washed like nearer waves above my head,
Like nearer waves of the dark sea of night,
   Almost against my face their raven spray,
   As down I followed by a narrow way.

XII.

I saw a garden full of flowers so bright,
     That emeralds set around deep ruby dyes,
And seed of pearl in golden agraffes pight,
     To them were dim; the lion's glowing eyes
Reflected on the tiger's head and tongue
     Were dim: with starry glow their dartles burst
     The night mists, and with purple grain traversed.

XIII.

I saw where some were red as glutted prong,
     To which the blood doth cling in ruddy beads,
Sanguinely gleaming, with jagged leaves and long,
     And whispered one another round the meads,
Which held in fiery travail all their wrath:
     I would have asked if they would wake all night,
     But got no answer, for to my affright

XIV.

Those were not crows: unto an inner path,
     Which greenly wound within the sanguine belt,
A shining serpent lured me; he his bath
     Chose in the coolest green, whose sweets he smelt,
And there beheld the gecko with his spots
     Move sideways underneath the crumbling frond,
     Where the white woody fibres blazed the bond

XV.

Hit in the scrannel wind-bit knees and knots;
  That serpent flew upon the gecko, swift
As evil thoughts do fly on evil thoughts:
  The lizard both its stings at once did lift
At head and tail; while, circling it, the lithe
  Wheel of the serpent surged and spun and quaked,
  The lizard shuddering like a body naked

XVI.

In hues of fear, which down his corse did writhe,
  Alternating in motion, till the snake
Struck, and the gecko stung, each almost blithe
  To feel the wounds such threatening could make.
Thus they two fought together, till I saw
  What I do say, that they did bite and clip
  And poison one another, till the whip

XVII.

Of fury wrought against their nature's law;
  Immingled each in each they lay deformed,
Each of his own dimension; then the maw
  Of the dragon 'gan to hiss, the snake outwormed
Into the dragon's head and double tail;
  Thus they transchanged their natures, and again
  The snake pursued, the gecko fled in vain.

2—2

XVIII.

Then from the venom, which did foam and fail
    Into the ground, my trembling eyeballs saw
A straight and pulp-leaved shoot spring up, and trail
    A hurtful form in the thick air, and draw
Its rankness to the rotten soil beneath:
    It grew with bristly spots of hair, whose tops
    Bore berries green, gathered in pending drops,

XIX.

In act to fall from out their careless sheath,
    Like caterpillars curled in greenish balls
Before they loose from plants their greedy teeth :
    This plant grew upwards as a serpent crawls,
And like a lizard was its lateral bend,
    And in its substance 'twas a man ; its face
    Dwelt upon wickedness, so crafty base,

XX.

I thought a mandrake would itself extend
    No other way from its old womb of earth ;
Then saw I that this belt of green did trend
    With growths no other than had had their birth
From the dull strife of those two venomed things :
    Very satyrs did they hurtle in the press,
    And shouldered one another motionless,

XXI.

Tempting me : one I grasped through all its stings,
  And crushed my hand into its pulpy cells ;
But soon drew back in horror, for two wings
  Whirred out and shrieked above me, and the bells
Wept in white tears, to which a thousand flies
  Flew, and would blacken them with swarming specks,
  Before the night could feel white tears to vex

XXII.

Her wicked heart : these wings whirred circle-wise
  Above me, and I cannot tell till now
What wings they were ; I give you this surmise,
  That they did spring out of the wounded bough,
As from Medusa's blood the father sprung
  Of half the Grecian fiends ; then did I flee
  From that green hideous belt, and sheltered me

XXIII.

In a white brake beyond a space of dung,
  Which wound within the green belt ; there I walked
Softly awhile before I felt the lung
  Of the deep night breathe on the lengthy stalked
Flowers, faintly faring in their families :
  As white were these as those I left were green,
  And bathed in pearl-white light ; and as the scene

XXIV.

Of the broad moon, o'erhanging its own rise,
    Were to be peopled by the swarming brood
Of larvas, lemures, and anatomies,
    Which should o'ercross her, and remain subdued,
Tortured and writhing in the searching beam;
    So saw I o'er these flowers so smoothly hewn
    A great light rising whiter than the moon,

XXV.

So did the fogs and mists take heart to gleam
    Round that white fire, but could not live upon 't;
So did the bats and owls leave their night theme
    And ramp and scream, but could not bear to haunt
Upon it, but whirred madly up and down,
    And all the ground was fell alive with snakes,
    So that great terror seized me in the brakes,

XXVI.

And I went forward towards that light'ning crown
    Over the innumerous ghostly flowers of night;
Until I reached it, and beheld full blown
    A mighty flower of flowers dressed in white,
In very heart of that translucent flame,
    Without one leaf it rose up from the ground,
    And gloriously issued in its white flower round.

XXVII.

Then even as I looked that flower became
A glorious lady, standing in meek pride,
Upon whose front, " called out of Misraim,"
I read, written in blood : " I am the Bride
W̦on by my knight Christ with the sword of wood,
The thorns, the nails, the spear." She spoke, and her
Two hands fell round the cross, her ransomer.

XXVIII.

Upon the lotus of her face I stood
Long meditating; while I scanned her robes
Of whitest samite, striped with stripes like blood,
And partly soiled with ashes, sad as Job's,
Whom Satan did reprove with many a stroke;
And all the seam was wrought with little crosses
Of brightest flame, which pierced little bosses

XXIX.

Of hearts that seemed like eyes, and wept and spoke.
Her form was beautiful and wondrous tall,
Her eyes were like half-moons in cloudy smoke,
Her height was as a pillar in a wall,
Her hair was as a flowery banner free,
Her glory like a fountain in the rocks,
Her graciousness like vines to tender flocks,

XXX.

Her eyes like lilies shaken by the bees,
   Her hair a net of moonbeams in a cloud,
Her thinness like a row of youngling trees,
   And golden bees hummed round her in a crowd,
And "pascit inter lilia," she sung.
   Her voice was as the sound of water borne
From draw-wells deep, and poured among the corn.

XXXI.

Then I, " Ah, loose to me that heavenly tongue,
   And tell me what it is that I have seen,
Ah, spouse, ah, sister of my Lord, upstrung
   In spirit have I reached the very queen,
As many times before in other scene
   Thou hast enlightened me with heavenly mien,
Now mayest thou also to thy servant deign.

XXXII.

" Now tell me what the triple belt doth mean,
   With the three kinds of flowers, red, green, and white ;
And wherefore dost thou tarry here, serene,
   Who mightest worship in the very height
Beside the rainbow, most blessed ?" She sung, " Behold
   I feed among the lilies, and they grow
Again, without the sense of any woe."

XXXIII.

With temperate joy her smile rose gently cold,
　As if the wind should bid a sough-reed work
Its circle-ripples in the water-wold ;
　" I am God's love in anguish in the mirk
Plains which the king of hell usurped, and hath ;
　And not my lilies do I comfort only,
　But every flower, bell-formed, long-leaved, or conely.

XXXIV.

" The ruddy flowers are sons of strife and wrath,
　Right seldom do they see the praise of God ;
The green flowers flourish but for Satan's swath,
　God doth not bid them occupy the sod :
Yet one time shall I dwell among them, fain
　To stay their greenness from its venom food,
　And Christ's true mysteries shall purge their blood.

XXXV.

" The white flowers are my children, by the rain
　Of blood and water nourished ; they are sad
And faint, thou seest ; but they have life in pain :
　Hereafter shalt thou view me pure and glad,
Yea, throned and gloried in the Seraphin,
　My ministers, who guard me in their guise ;
　Christ's body hath chief glory in the skies."

XXXVI.

Those golden bees, which all this time within
　　Reach of her balmy breath clung murmuringly,
Like dance of gnats, which in the morning spin
　　Their maze beneath some widely spreading tree,
In spite of all the spider's cruel eyes,
　　And dare not venture forth their wanderings
　　Lest the new air should damp their gauzy wings.

XXXVII.

These golden bees in such a wondrous wise
　　Did now increase their lustre, and about
That dame did flash such splendid ministries,
　　And spun with such swift motion, that their rout
Dazzled her from my eyesight clean away ;
　　Nor aught could I discern a little space,
　　But groped in darkness, with a stumbling pace

XXXVIII.

Leaving that spot and tottering on my way,
　　Until I felt my garment drag behind
Over rough stones; and there knelt I to pray,
　　And there the freshness of a river wind
Rise to my face, and on my hands and knees
　　I leaned, and felt cold water creep along,
　　Up to my wrists, the while a mighty gong

XXXIX.

Burst awfully from out the very breeze :
    At length I could look up, and to a sea
Of fire wavetops ; not wavetops of these seas
    Ægean, white wavetops or black ; the lee
Shore where I stood received a fiery train
    Of phosphor billows, which did seethe so free,
    They made that river boundless as the sea.

XL.

Then leaped I in, impelled by secret pain ;
    This was the way in which I won the heaven ;
The many billows heard my breath complain,
    Then bore me downwards with a mighty steven :
Like a pale man just dead, in peace my corse
    Rolled downwards like a log o'ercharged with weeds
    To where the widening river bed recedes

XLI.

Into the ocean ; there the tidal force
    Cast me upon this island lone and drear,
When as I oped mine eyes I saw the course
    Of heaven begin: a mountain rose i' the air
Cut with strict stairs of jasper, and along
    Its windings downwards coming did I see
    A heavenly throng in glorious panoply.

XLII.

Yea, that great glory sweeping in a throng
  Of aureoles before me; saints were there
Bowed till their wings o'ercrossed them; while a song
  Streamed from their lips apart, which never were
Stirred from that curve of rapture tremulous;
  And they rose heads o'er heads, on high, on high,
  Gold, golden glory, to the verge of sky;

XLIII.

From which they issued multitudinous;
  Wherein appeared a glow of ruby bright,
And clear sweet sapphire; 'twas the very house
  Of veiling; whence on all the raiment white,
On golden glories and on golden hair
  Spread thickly like a golden fleece about
  On virgin shoulders, and so threaded out

XLIV.

On lilies with their gold crowns crumbled fair,
  And solemn leaves curled with some thought severe,
Or heads bowed forward with the weight of prayer,
  On heads uplifted backwards to revere,
Streamed forth a mighty blessing from above,
  Streamed forth a splendour from the ruby red,
  And a great pureness from the sapphire dread.

XLV.

Ranged row on row they come ; the light of love
  Burned softly in their eyes, row ranged on row
Of men in heavenly panoply, a grove
  Of violet plumes and lifted swords; below
And-through, 'twixt arm and shoulder, and between
  Plumed helm and helm, wild eyes and golden hair
And passionate lips ; with throngings here and there,

XLVI.

The goodly people of that heavenly queen,
  Blessedest, sweetest, holiest, fairest, all ;
Unto me and below me as I ween,
  Whilst I beyond them upwards to the wall
Of heaven did gaze, where as if unawares
  A mystery passed in the light of light
Along the whole length of the heaven's height.

XLVII.

The wall rose solemnly in many squares,
  Of scarlet brick, above a moated space
Of water clear ; and by unending stairs
  This company was crossing to my place,
Their splendours ever reaching lower and lower,
  I gazing higher and higher, for my chin
An angel lifted, and 'twas from within

XLVIII.

His golden wings that veiled his sight that hour,
  That I too looked and saw a mystery
Proceed, while mightily shone out the flower
  Of the gold wings upon the violet sky,
Came in their battles, all the seraphim
    With giant plumes, with glory-beaming eyes,
    Long bands and wrapping robes, in solemn guise,

XLIX.

Came Michael, and an army followed him;
  His sword, two-handed, carried he before,
His vast eyes on the hilt, his shield's broad rim
  Swung half of it behind him; in the score
Of his knights followed all the cherubim;
    And half the stars shone in his banner wide
    And in it all the winds were multiplied.

L.

Came Gabriel, with his banner over him,
  White lilies, brass-bright flowers, and leaves of green;
A lily, too, he carried seemed to brim,
  With golden flames, which mounted pure and clean
To touch his blessed mouth, and then would trim
    Themselves within the lily leaf again:
    Gabriel's fair head sank even with dream-pain

LI.

Came Raphael, and an army followed him;
   His staff was in his hand, as he strode on;
His gourd was slung behind; one mighty limb
   Showed itself bare in passing; and upon
His track came many a knightly palmer grim:
   On horses these, their horses well beseen
   As those who fight on earth for heaven's queen.

LII.

Came Uriel, and his banner over him—
   Red-pointed flames that lightened on the field
Of steadfast judgment, sapphirine, till dim
   The eyesight, and the brain behind it reeled;
Behind him walked the strong robed seraphim;
   A roll and book in his two hands he bore,
   At which great trembling all my entrails tore.

LIII.

Came Chamuel, and his banner over him,
   Half red, half blue, and barred with golden bars;
Upon a seat of cloud he seemed to swim,
   Red, yellow, grey, and passed across the stars;
Across his knees, in both his hands, a slim,
   Long quivering rod, with sword leaves at the end;
   Chamuel went swiftly, seeming to ascend.

LIV.

Came Jophiel, and an army followed him :
  In his right hand a sword gleamed sharp and clear,
Whose edge he felt with his left hand, and grim
  Smiled he to find it biting very sheer ;
His thousands thronged behind of seraphim,
  Armed likewise all ; his fiery footsteps cleft
  The little white clouds on the pathway weft.

LV.

Come Zadkiel, and an army followed him;
  Closed were their hands, and wings half shut to sail:
Grey and much crimson seemed their vesture, dim,
  Much like a dream, as when the light doth fail
In melancholy wrack and crimson bar
  Above a storm; his army flitted on
  Like falling leaves; some sadness, all were gone.

LVI.

These all went solemnly, as if to war;
  The seven archangels, with his army each;
They drifted in their march away, till far
  In the blind sky together in one reach,
Like a great flight of birds: I watching, saw
  Their great pavilions set far off like palls,
  Beyond the utmost circle of heaven's walls.

LVII.

High to the west three cloudlike palls I saw;
 The highest, foamy flakes of gray and rose;
The next long strips of blue with saffron flaw;
 The last of gray, and over it clear glows
Of yellow vapour: 'neath them all a vast
 Blue lake, and under it a long grey shore,
 And so another lake, paler; then more

LVIII.

Of long gray shore, with pale fire-fringe, that passed
 Beneath it, folding in another lake
Of water blue; and to grim hills at last,
 Whose upper parts were white with many a flake
Of shining lava; and their slopes were gray,
 And ended in the earth with one great wild
 Border of lurid sulphur triply piled.

LIX.

Thither did all God's angels pass away,
 And then a voice cried, Woe, Jerusalem:
And by this time I saw myself; I say,
 Could see myself the way that I saw them,
Drawn by my two arms upwards, lifted straight
 Upward, and laid upon a thick red cloud,
 Like blood soaked into snow, and overbowed

LX.

By horrid frost, and bruised by heavy weight:
How weak was I with visions, O Lord God,
Not having eaten for so long ! my fate
Alone of men to quake beneath the rod
Of coming woes ; yea still to gaze and hear
The four beasts answer even where I lay,
And great cloud angels rend themselves away

LXI.

From the four corners of my cloudy bier:
Above which rose the great white throne, and shook
And muttered like a cauldron: deadly near
It was; and straight the senses all forsook
This trunk ; like as when foam spreads heavily
On tides, some spume clings in a small shore-bay
Some little time, so clung I where I lay.

LXII.

I and my cloud : the rest was mystery.
Oh, humble heart, forbear to speak at all;
Yet verily the love-beam beamed on me.
Then like a rainbow did that lady call,—
" For ever shalt thou teach God's love to man
In wondrous fulness both of joy and pain,
Apostle of the Lamb that once was slain,

LXIII.

" And prophet thou !—apostle, thou dost scan
   The round of love in triple period,
Prophet—not any prophet is so wan—
   Tell out the vials of the wrath of God."
I gather that beyond these coasts Ægean
   Beyond this little world of Greeks, where nought
   But man exists, nor knowledge save of thought,

LXIV.

The throne of love waves in the empyrean,
   In angel clouds, flame hues, sharp crystal wracks ;
In mountain spears uplifted as a pæan,
   In mighty rivers sent through golden tracks,
In lands unknown, where, yet a little while
   And men shall pray: lo, now, a sorrow-smile,
   The purple cloud swells over isle and isle.

St. Peter.

———◆◇◆———

Thou brightness of the everlasting light,
Unspotted mirror of the power divine,
    Wisdom and Word, thou Son of God,
    My heart is broken like a clod,
    My tears are falling on the sod,
    Whereas through this long period,
                                    Says sorrow,

They all forsook Thee, and alike we fled;
Ah, how am I so much behind them all?
    Thy Master, ah, thy thrice denied,
    Even now they shall have crucified;
    Wherefore this sobbing may divide
    The weight thou feelest in heart and side,
                                    Says sorrow.

John saith that they who love do fear the most;
In truth, that very love makes faint and weak;
    The truest sometimes fail the most;
    He left Thee in that traitor host,
    When torches frayed the olive coast,
    The olives witnessing, "Thou know'st,"
                                    In darkness.

Saith Philip, that the mortal body weighs
The spirit with much trouble to the earth;
    The senses flatter and perplex,
    And lust the understanding wrecks,
    This œnomel the false flower decks,
    Whose sweets rise up through waxen necks
              In darkness.

Lazarus says he saw a hand stretch forth
From end to end of heaven instantly;
    And holy beams were working out
    Great scrolls that lightened all about,
    The mighty sky, which seemed, in doubt,
    To darken inwards, but without
              To glory.

And on these beams a glory suddenly
Rose in the heaven of heavens immeasured height,
    Which brightened them as if upon
    Some plain of dædal flowers, which spun
    Darkly within the wind, the sun
    Had paled, and then at once begun
              To glory.

This comforts me the most, O Master great,
Oh, worker ever, as it may be seen,
    In anguish, as Thou dost fulfil
    Composedly the mighty will,
    Which pierceth as a mighty drill
    The fashions of the ages, till
            Through ages

The one design connects : ah, still the sod
Bids me drain out my tears and wash it through ;
    O Lord, it bids mine eyes renew   ,
    Their sorrow, for thine eyes so true,
    As the sad rain might mesh the hue
    Of flowers tenderer than grew
                    Through ages.

Sadly the grassy sod sobs to the leaves ;
Come down to me, and I will bury you ;
    In my deep bosom·ye shall lie ;
    Too long ye wave and flag on high ;
    The dews drop softly from the sky
    Like syllables, " weep, weep, and die ;"
                    The leaves fall.

The little trefoils twinkle their sweet eyes ;
The little banks of grass together thrust
    With shrivelled points, will never tear you,
    On their small poignards they shall bear you,
    Frittered like flame their points shall spare you,
    The binding weed shall gently snare you
                    (The leaves fall)

Down to my fresh moss heart, where ye shall watch
Your scarlet purple mother branches gleam ;
    While worm and emmet work anon,
    To trace in each its skeleton,
    And all heaven's curdling clouds roll on
    O'er fruits which, lurid, sanguine, dun,
                    (The leaves fall,)

Droop lower and lower towards me: ah, come down,
Ye stay and flutter all too long ! the fig
    Swoops in large circles, and where frets
    The anxious vine, she sadly sets
    The ashy spider with his nets
    To do her watching while she lets
                The leaves fall.

The hoary nightshade drops her berries here,
The tragacanth with purple eyelids weeps,
    The ivy-thorn his leaves depends
    To where the comfort woodbine wends
    To rescue from the briar her friends;
    'Tis sadly thinking for what ends
                'Twas borrowed.

For my Lord's brow—my tears fall last of all ;
My bitter weeping closes up the night ;
    I cannot hear, I weep so sore
    The thorn lamenting evermore
    To thin leaves stirring on the floor
    Of moss that trembles to the core,
                'Twas borrowed.

Yet have I secret comforts in my soul,
I think my soul finds comfort in strange ways,
    Where others would but die, or sink
    Depth after depth from the first brink
    Of sinning; this, as I must think,
    Doth distance me at least a link
                From others,

From traitorous mouths which do but hide the truth,
As clouds that hold no water hide the heavens,
    And slip from guilt to guilt like beasts   '
    In tracks, as Pharisees and priests,
    Who strive the greatest's, not the least's,
    Sedile to occupy at feasts
               From others.

Then jostle one another and devour;
So these composed souls, being set one way,
    If they transgress, pursue the wrong
    Sleekly from guile to guile along
    A path well downwards, in a throng—
    So common 'tis—like swine the prong
               Drives onward

Without reprieve; they do but overbear
The one course which their nature gave at first,
    While I, though in me was made breach,
    Because I hate them, rally reach;
    I fell before their hoot and screech,
    Because I hate the ways that each
               Drives onward.

Oh, coward, coward, coward!   But this I know,
That love in God is goodness, and in Christ
    That love is mercy, and in man
    That love is sorrow; I shall plan,
    Unplan, and grasp, and gasp, and scan,
    From this my life out; who shall ban
               My sorrow?

Not earth that drinks my tears ; not heavenly sky,
Not they who took with me the bread and wine;
    Perhaps not God who looks on me,
    The Father, thinking of the tree
    Of cursing in me rooted, see
    The flinders ; not the victim, He,
                  My sorrow !

St. Mary Magdalene.

Kneeling before the altar step,
  Her white face stretched above her hands;
In one great line her body thin
Rose robed right upwards to her chin;
Her hair rebelled in golden bands,
    And filled her hands;

Which likewise held a casket rare
  Of alabaster at that tide;
Simeon was there and looked at her,
Trancedly kneeling, sick and fair;
Three parts the light her features tried,
    She rest implied.

Strong singing reached her from within,
  Discordant, but with weighty rhymes;
Her swaying body kept the stave;
Then all the woods about her wave,
She heard, and saw, in mystic mimes,
    Herself three times.

Once, in the doorway of a house,
  With yellow lintels painted fair,
Very far off, where no men pass,
Green and red banners hung in mass
Above scorched woodwork wormed and bare,
  And spider's snare.

She, scarlet in her form and gold,
  Fallen down upon her hands and knees,
Her arms and bosom bare and white,
Her long hair streaming wild with light,
Felt all the waving of the trees,
  And hum of bees.

A rout of mirth within the house,
  Upon the ear of madness fell,
Stunned with its dread, yet made intense ;
A moment, and might issue thence
Upon the prey they quested well,
  Seven fiends of hell.

She grovelled on her hands and knees,
  She bit her breath against that rout ;
Seven devils inhabited within,
Each acting upon each his sin,
Limb locked in limb, snout turning snout,
  And these would out.

Twice, and the woods lay far behind,
   Gold corn spread broad from slope to slope;
The copses rounded in faint light,
Far from her pathway gleaming white,
Which gleamed and wound in narrow scope,
   Her narrow hope.

She on the valley stood and hung,
   Then downward swept with steady haste;
The steady wind behind her sent
Her robe before her as she went;
Descending on the wind, she chased
   The form she traced.

She, with her blue eyes blind with flight,
   Rising and falling in their cells,
Hands held as though she played a harp,
Teeth glistening as in laughter sharp,
Flew ghostly on, a strength like hell's,
   When it rebels.

Behind her, flaming on and on,
   Rushing and streaming as she flew;
Moved over hill as if through vale,
Through vale as if o'er hill, no fail;
Her bosom trembled as she drew
   Her long breath through.

Thrice, with an archway overhead,
    Beneath, what might have seemed a tomb ;
White garments fallen fold on fold,
As if limbs yet were in their hold,
Drew the light further in the gloom,
    Of the dark room.

She, fallen without thought or care,
    Heard, as it were, a ceaseless flow
Of converse muttered in her ear,
Like waters sobbing wide and near,
About things happened long ago
    Of utter woe.

The Holy Mother at the Cross.

Of Mary's pains may now learn whoso will,
    When she stood underneath the groaning tree
Round which the true Vine clung : three hours the mill
    Of hours rolled round ; she saw in visions three
The shadows walking underneath the sun,
    And these seemed all so very faint to be,
That she could scarcely tell how each begun,
    And went its way, minuting each degree
That it existed on the dial stone :
    For drop by drop of wine unfalteringly,
Not stroke by stroke in blood, the three hours gone
    She seemed to see.

Three hours she stood beneath the cross ; it seemed
    To be a wondrous dial stone, for while
Upon the two long arms the sunbeams teemed,
    So was the head-piece like a centre stile ;
Like to the dial where the judges sat
    Upon the grades, and the king crowned the pile,
In Zion town, that most miraculous plat
    On which the shadow backward did defile ;

And now towards the third hour the sun enorme
    Dressed up all shadow to a bickering smile
I' the heat, and in its midst the form of form
    Lay like an isle.

Because that time so heavily beat and slow
    That fancy in each beat was come and gone;
Because that light went singing to and fro,
    A blissful song in every beam that shone;
Because that on the flesh a little tongue
    Instantly played, and spake in lurid tone;
Because that saintly shapes with harp and gong
    Told the three hours, whose telling made them one;
Half hid, involved in alternating beams,
    Half mute, they held the plectrum to the zone,
Therefore, as God her senses shield, it seems
    A dial stone.

Three hours she stood beside the cross; it seemed
    A splendid flower; for red dews on the edge
Stood dropping; petals doubly four she deemed
    Shot out like steel knives from the central wedge,
Which quadranted their perfect circle so
    As if four anthers should a vast flower hedge
Into four parts, and in its bosom, lo,
    The form lay, as the seed-heart holding pledge
Of future flowers; yea, in the midst was borne
    The head low drooped upon the swollen ledge
Of the torn breast; there was the ring of thorn;
    This flower was fledge.

Because her woe stood all about her now,
 No longer like a stream as ran the hour ;
Because her cleft heart parted into two,
 No more a mill-wheel spinning to time's power ;
Because all motion seemed to be suspense ;
 Because one ray did other rays devour ;
Because the sum of things rose o'er her sense,
 She standing 'neath its dome as in a bower ;
Because from one thing all things seemed to spume,
 As from one mouth the fountain's hollow shower ;
Therefore it seemed His and her own heart's bloom,
 A splendid flower.

Now it was finished ; shrivelled were the leaves
 Of that pain-flower, and wasted all its bloom,
She felt what she had felt then ; as receives,
 When heaven is capable, the cloudy stroom
The edge of the white garment of the moon ;
 So felt she that she had received that doom ;
And as an outer circle spins in tune,
 Born of the inner on the sky's wide room,
Thinner and wider, that doom's memories,
 Broken and thin and wild, began to come
As soon as this : St. John unwrapt his eyes,
 And led her home.

Poems.

—◆—

A Lenten Mystery.

⸳ FIDES IN DEO OPTIMA.

In the dread Patmos of the town
I heard a voice from heaven come down;
Then found me in a desert place
Of kneaded clay-field, poor and base,
With a crowd flowing at its edge.
Then did the voice great things allege
Against the town in bitter rhyme.

The Voice.

God his eternity on time,
God his infinity on space,
Casts: God proceeds in all earth's ways,
In all that He hath made God lurks,
He waiteth man in all his works:

4

Dost thou in anywise observe
His presence as the living nerve
Of life, and dost thou reverence
For His sake every form of sense,
And strive to take each for thine own ?

JONAH.

We answer not, we know not ; one
With twisted eyes of blue I saw
Look this way for a moment; awe
Lowered for a moment half his lids,
But he knows not; that other bids
Thee mock thyself with what he is,
Being a fiend with infamies
Unnumbered eating up his soul ;
But all know nothing, in the whole
Mass of them is not one that knows.

THE VOICE.

How mightily heaven overflows,
How countlessly doth God indite
Himself in darkness and in light,
And all that grows between these two—
Star-formed, and written on the blue
Void of the all-embracing shade—
Shade-formed, and solemnly inlaid
Between bright forms of life that crawl
In and out the mother womb of all
The solemn all-embracing shade.

JONAH.   ·

We know not, Lord, what Thou hast said,
Ah, what, O Lord, can these men know ?

THE VOICE.

God *seemed* as man long time ago,
His going was in Eden heard
Among the trees, his presence scared
Blood-shedding Cain ; again, again
God *felt* as man, felt human pain,
And pity, wrath, and jealousy ;
God *spake* as man, this finally :
The Word made flesh among us dwelt,
Great glory from the heavens did melt
Into the blood of human kings.

JONAH.

Ah, now we wake, yet the lie clings
Sordidly, makes the truth a lie.

THE VOICE.

Which three things live continually,
God seemed as man, yea felt, yea lived ;
Still, still God walketh undeceived
About the Eden of his earth,
And still holds solemn wrath or mirth
At things which happen in this time ;

·   4—2

And still He liveth in man's clime,
And speaketh words which do remain;
Christ-God hath come to make them plain,
Christ-God, to seal this sacrament.

JONAH.

Alive now ?   What is their intent ?
Crossing their thumbs with writhing lips,
And eyes set grimly.   One upwhips
His arm-long club, and fell and full
Closes upon the shaggy skull
Of his own ass, already cut
To the white bone.

THE VOICE.

This doth outshut
All infinites, that Christ left His,
Yet brings it to His sacrifice,
(O mystery of mysteries,
Leaving His infinities,
And entering into space and time,
The Godhead !) this transcends sublime,
That through man's nature He transfuse
What soul and corpse alike renews,
The perfect God and perfect Man !

JONAH.

Now this enrages, who can scan
Such rage, and us not hate therefore ?

THE VOICE.

All-loving life, He doth restore
Through man's own spirit-spring of faith,
What man himself hath lost in death,
The life eternal, incorrupt,
Which He, all-living love, once scooped
From His own being, which remains
Sunk, but not lost, amid the pains
Of death long dying, which revives
Under His cordials, breaks its gyves,
Adds to itself all forms of life.

JONAH.

Ah, foully we express our strife,
Ah, sicklily we grow malign.

THE VOICE.

And stands at last, complex and fine,
A perfect man, recovered all,
And strong, yea, strong enough to fall
Full-breasted on the Infinite.
Know ye these issues, feel their light,
Breaking from far for those who sit
In darkness; how that Christ doth knit
In love to love the life once lost?
Rage, chafe ye then, because this most
Solemn of things in light is lit?

JONAH.

Behold a mountain, chasm-split,
Pine-darkened, ashen with white snows;
In every gash a snow-stream flows,
A snow-veil slowly breaks and weeps,
A snow-rock ghostly wakes and sleeps;
Bears limp along its pathless snow,
Along its deserts white wolves go,
Like flights of ravens in the air;
I see four men come forth and glare
From grisly caverns where they lie:
These gave Christ-God his agony—
Pontius Pilatus, and Judas,
Herodes, Caiaphas.

JUDAS ISCARIOTES, CAIAPHAS, PONTIUS PILATUS, HERODES.

JUDAS.

Take thou this money, Caiaphas,
I pray thee now for shame, whereas
Thou hast betrayed me; I, alas,
　　My Master dear betrayed.

CAIAPHAS.

Much gold to many paid I when
I was made priest, to many men;
To thee for Christ but pieces ten
　　Of silver thrice I paid.

PONTIUS PILATUS.

One came and begged his body here
To lay it in a sepulchre;
I granted freely his desire,
    And they have buried him.

HERODES.

It is great marvel he is dead;
Three years ago he came and said
That he went up to lay his head
    Within Jerusalem.

Eunice.

———◦◦◦———

WHEN her holy life was ended
   Eunice lay upon her side ;
When her holy death was ended
   Eunice died.

Then a spirit raised her spirit
   From the urn of dripping tears ;
And a spirit from her spirit
   Soothed the fears.

And upon her spirit lightly—
   Spirit upon spirit-wrote ;
And she rose to worlds eternal,
   Taking note.

First she joined the world eternal
   Which is never seen of men ;
Through its climes she wandered lightly,
   Happy then.

Then she learned a song of comfort
  For the loves she left behind,
Children kissing one another,
  Husband kind.

I have joined the world of spirit,
  Which the flesh does never see;
But to you a realm is open
  As to me.

World invisible of spirit
  Doth invisible remain
Not less certainly to angels
  Than to men.

As you see it not on earth
  I behold it not in heaven;
Yet to both of us alike
  It is given.

For we both may walk within it,
  And meet blindfolded above;
'Tis the world of thought and feeling
  And of love.

Enter then this world of spirit;
  It is yours by right of birth,
Mine by death: let heaven possess it,
  And let earth.

Dream.

I.

With camel's hair I clothed my skin,
  I fed my mouth with honey wild ;
And set me scarlet wool to spin,
  And all my breast with hyssop filled ;
Upon my brow and cheeks and chin
  A bird's blood spilled.

I took a broken reed to hold,
  I took a sponge of gall to press ;
I took weak water-weeds to fold
  About my sacrificial dress.

I took the grasses of the field,
  The flax was bolled upon my crine ;
And ivy thorn and wild grapes healed
  To make good wine.

I took my scrip of manna sweet,
  My cruse of water did I bless ;
I took the white dove by the feet,
  And flew into the wilderness.

II.

The tiger came and played ;
Uprose the lion in his mane ;
The jackal's tawny nose
And sanguine dripping tongue
Out of the desert rose
And plunged its sands among;
The bear came striding o'er the desert plain.

Uprose the horn and eyes
And quivering flank of the great unicorn,
And galloped round and round;
Uprose the gleaming claw
Of the leviathan, and wound
In steadfast march did draw
Its course away beyond the desert's bourn.

I stood within a maze
Woven round about me by a magic art,
And ordered circle-wise:
The bear more near did tread,
And with two fiery eyes,
And with a wolfish head,
Did close the circle round in every part.

III.

With scarlet corded horn,
With frail wrecked knees and stumbling pace,
The scapegoat came :
His eyes took flesh and spirit dread in flame
At once, and he died looking towards my face.

The Wizard's Funeral.

For me, for me, two horses wait,
Two horses stand before my gate:
Their vast black plumes on high are cast,
Their black manes swing in the midnight blast,
Red sparkles from their eyes fly fast.
But can they drag the hearse behind,
Whose black plumes mystify the wind?
What a thing for this heap of bones and hair!
Despair, despair!
Yet think of half the world's winged shapes
Which have come to thee wondering:
At thee the terrible idiot gapes,
At thee the running devil japes,
And angels stoop to thee and sing
From the soft midnight that enwraps
Their limbs, so gently, sadly fair;—
Thou seest the stars shine through their hair.
The blast again, ho, ho, the blast!
I go to a mansion that shall outlast;
And the stoled priest who steps before
Shall turn and welcome me at the door.

Reflection.

THERE are two natures make one soul :
  The sea with many floods,
  The earth with countless woods :
      Bring the waves of the sea,
      Sings the earth, unto me ;
      Bring the waves of the tree
      Unto me, says the sea.

There are two halves that make the whole :
  The heaven with clouds that drops,
  The earth with mountain tops,
      Crying, Give me of the cloud
      My nakedness to shroud,
      While the heaven replies as loud,
      Let me rest each cloud—each cloud.

And what art thou, O Death ?
For thou seemest to gather breath
    From the crystal spasm
        Of the mountain,
    Leaving bare a chasm
        White and lonely as a fountain.

Sea from land—what remain ?
Desert cavern, arid plain,
And the tears that pour
From the tottering shore.

Heaven from earth—
What result has birth ?
Earth is made hell,
Is heaven made earth ?

Thou art sprung from the writhing
Of the lonely low or high thing;
And, O Death, thou art cursed
To be last, or to be first.

The Soul's World.

ART thou standing on the shore
Which the spirits tremble o'er,
Ere they take the plunge for ever
In the bottomless receiver:
This commencing dissidence
Ere it cleave us hence and hence;
Ere the first hour stays its sands
Since the life-pulse left thy hands;
Art thou there, and dost thou cast
Thy strange glance, the first and last,
On the world which thou didst fill
With thy essence: on my will—
'Twas an ocean, and its tide
Ruled by thee: therein did ride
Fruitful reason—'twas an isle
Rendered happy by thy smile;
On each process of my brain
'Twas the travailing in pain
Of creations which uprose,
Founded each on other's close;

On my hopes, my joys, my pains;—
These were mountains, valleys, plains;
On my intellect which fed ;—
'Twas a river's sinuous head
Eating out into the sea:
On my spirit's entity ;
Which embraced as its own essence
Thy whole mystery of presence;—
'Twas the full and rounded sphere
In its ether bright and clear.
Many a chasm in this thy world
Mayest thou view in crystal furled,
Many a rent and gristly knot,
Many a melting lava grot,
Many a white and ghastly waste
In thy smiling garden placed,
Many an earthquake catching breath
From the savage fires beneath.
Many a seam of pain and crime,
Much of wreck and much of time.
Ah, sweet soul of all, then turn
From the dark things thou must descern ;
Quit me not in hate for ever,
Plunge not in the deathless river
Of the bottomless receiver.

The Wanderer.

―――◦◊◦―――

I.

Oh, that remote and lonely shore,
 Between the river and the sea,
 Towards which my boat was drifting me.
Never again, oh, nevermore
 Let me behold it: 'tis the grave
Of a cast nature; yet I have
 Dream times to think of it, and feel
How sweet beneath its cirque of trees
 The islet lay! The sunbeams stole
Downwards, and strove to uncongeal
 The voiceless magic which did weave
The lonely island to my soul.
 The sunset crowned its cirque of trees,
Upon its limbs did shadow cleave,
 And round its sloping terraces
 The mists curled like a lawny frieze.

5

II.

My shallop parted the tall rushes,
    The boat's head rustled through the flags ;
        I was alone,
        All, all were gone ;
        Dead ere its prime,
        The morning time;
        Strange bearded men
        Were out of ken ;
        I had rowed with them
            Up the river amain ;
        I had fled from them
            Down the river again.
    I grasped the overhanging bushes,
    And drew myself upon the crags.

III.

I came beside a still lagoon
    Of inky blackness, whereupon,
Like a lake-lily, lay the moon,
    White, ere her reign of gold begun.

IV.

I came through vales of level flowers,
    Sunstruck with glory o'er the grass,
    Clipped by the winds and the mists in a mass,
And silkily, sulkily, hued for the showers.

V.

I looked upon the wildness blooming,
At thronging stems to distance looming,
Dim-outlined shadows nearer coming,
Dark foliage, more darkly glooming.

VI.

Then said I, " Every day will bring
    From the wide rolling of the waves,
    From the warm breathing of the winds,
Some fresh delight, some newer thing,
    And nature will increase in kinds,
And I will be her king.
    ·   Yes ; field, and rock, and flower, and tree,
        Shall with my presence peopled be,
        As with a deeper entity.

VII.

I had been passion-seared, and tost
    On the blind waves of accident ;
Had played with chance and always lost,
    Had loved, and been heart-shent ;
Had tasted pleasure's after-pain,
    Had looked for sweet, and found but gall,
Had wrestled with my fellow-men,
    And risen baffled from the fall :
        I said, I here will have abode,
        Where never foot of man hath trod.

VIII.

And I will love all beauty here,
But beauty shall be everywhere ;
   And over all my love shall change,
Shall flit and hover ceaselessly,
   And broaden with its wider range,
Always intense, but wildly free ;
   But never will I seek return
For equal love so widely spent,
   Oh, never, never let me burn
With special passion in me pent !

IX.

I had fled away, ere my heart should change,
   From the men who hated me more and more ;
      They toiled afloat
      In their labouring boat,
      In their solemn copes,
      With their arms like ropes :
      They sat in their ranks
      On the rowing planks,
      And they rose and fell
      To the time of the oar ;
      Black eyes and curt hair;
      Black eyes watched me well
      On wave and on shore,
         Everywhere !

I had fled away that my heart might range,
  From the unendurable sorrow it bore.
    Now very stilly
    Lay the lake lily,
    And not so chilly
    The covert hilly;
    The meadow rilly
    Was not so chilly.
I had fled away with the presage strange,
  Of rest to be won on a secret shore.

X.

Through forests wide I wandered,
Where large-leaved flowers had grown to head,
Where fluctuated endless shade.

XI.

And everywhere my human sense,
Fraught with its dread intelligence,
Worked with the power reflected thence.

XII.

I said, " These rocks, and trees, and flowers
  Have grown and changed, but still remained
Mere daughters of the suns and showers,
  Most beautiful, but ne'er have gained
The presence of a human soul,

They know not pity, they know not dole,
 They know not passion's mystery.
Lo ! I am here a human soul,
And I will clothe them in human stole,
Will give to each most subtle reach
 Of sorrow and of sympathy."

XIII.

So day by day I wrought my will
 Upon wide nature's open face;
My thought informed each particle
 Of being throughout all the place;
For day by day, when the great sun
 Was greatest, would I keep the shade
Of rocky hollows in the dun
 And sleepy light by lichen made,
And there my thoughts would truant run,
 While wreaths of fancy round me played.

XIV.

But when the dews had fallen soft,
 And night had fallen on the dews;
And when the moon was far aloft,
 Then forth I wandered, not to lose
The thoughtfulness of brooding rest,
 For still emotive power would ooze
From the full feelings of my breast;
 But forth I went through dell and croft,
Through all the gloom from east to west.

XV.

Oft by the marsh's quaggy edge
  I heard the wind-swept rushes fall;
Where through an overgrowth of sedge
  Rolled the slow mere funereal:
I heard the music of the leaves
  Unto the night wind's fingering,
I saw the dropping forest eaves
  Make in the mere their water-ring.

XVI.

And so I fared, until, upstaying
  My thoughts on richer blooms, that gained
My eyes, and thence no further straying,
  Whole solemn hours have I remained,
Wreaths of fine fancies round me playing,
  With advents strange and vanishings;
Half in my inmost soul delaying,
  Half bodied upon outer things.

XVII.

But day by day about the marge
  Of this slow-brooding dreaminess,
The shadow of the past lay large,
  And brooded low and lustreless;
Then vanished as I looked on it,
  Yet back returned with wider sweep,
And broad upon my soul would sit,
  Like a storm-cloud above the deep.

XVIII.

Yea, subtle, word-banned memories,
   Heart-surges of black bitterness,
Untouched by sorrow's softer dyes,
   About my brain would throng and press:
I found I could not alchemize
   And purge away the dross of facts,
And I was mad for human cries,
   For human sorrows, human acts.

XIX.

" I see," I cried, "the waste of waves,
   That shifts from out the western tracts;
I see the sun that ever laves
   With liquid gold their cataracts;
And night by night I see the moon
   Career and thwart the waves of cloud;
I see great nature burgeon
   Through all her seasons, laughter-browed.
But what are these things unto me?
   They lack not me, they are full-planned.
I must have love in my degree,
   A human heart, a human hand;
For oh ! 'tis better far to share,
   Though life all dark, all bitter be,
With human bosoms human care:"
   I launched my boat upon the sea.

The Pilgrim of Love.

WHAT I had seen a far-away white cloud
So long, had grown a mountain by the morn;
A thousand torrents at its feet were loud,
And rolled one volume o'er its lowest horn,

Which gloried like one whitened wave of sea;
And far above the mountain crags were pitched,
Like a white mocking hand which beckoned me
In gesture, answered by the boat's prow twitched

Back o'er the lake, leaving me standing there
Alone upon the taunting mountain shore:
Now for my life, methought; and first my care
Was given to tread the shattered valley o'er,

With its rude waste of stones like lions couched
Upon the desert; then I reached, indeed,
The mountain, where its mighty spur debouched,
A vast earth dragon, whose coils half recede

Into the bowels of its awful mother ;
  And on its bulk my little pathway wound;   ‘
Point after point of grisly light did smother
  The horror which they could not fully sound.

And I ascended till I met the wrath
  Of white snow, dabbled on the gnashing teeth
Of slate rocks in the avalanche's path ;
  Then stayed, and looked above, and looked beneath.

Above—stand up the crystal spears of rock,
  Heaven's army, ever charging into light,
Retreating into cloud ; not less than flock
  Of dreadful angels from the Sapphirine height ;

And not in that frank mystery, pretence
  Of wing or palm, or radiant hands or feet :
I see the clear-aired crystal, and the sense
  Of spiritual presence grows complete.

Below—two figures in the morning mist
  Move up for ever to the mountain's shoulder,
On which my rest is settled ; then they list,
  To fade for ever over spur and boulder.

I cannot track the light within their eyes,
  I cannot track the marching of their feet ;
I only know, whenever they arise,
  The sense of human presence grows complete.

Dawning.

—◦—

OVER the hill I have watched the dawning,
I have watched the dawn of morning light,
Because I cannot well sleep by night,
Every day I have watched the dawning.
And to-day very early my window shook
With the cold wind fresh from the ghastly brook,
And I left my bed to watch the dawning.
Very cold was the light, very pale, very still,
And the wind blew great clouds over the hill
Towards the wet place of the dying dawning;
It blew them over towards the east
In heavier charge as the light increased,
From the very death of the dying dawning.
Whence did the clouds come over the hill?
I cannot tell, for no clouds did fill
The clear space opposite the dawning
Right over the hill, long, low, and pearl-grey,
Set in the wind to live as it may;

And as the light increased from the dawning,
The cold, cold brook unto my seeming
Did intermit its ghastly gleaming
And ran forth brighter in the dawning.
The wall-fruit stretched along the wall,
The pear-tree waved its banners tall;
Then close beside me in the dawning,
I saw thy face so stonily grey,
And the close lips no word did say,
The eyes confessed not in the dawning.
I saw a man ride through the light
Upon the hill-top, out of sight
Of me and thee and all the dawning.

The Sole Survivor.

BLOOD, blood, blood in the morning sky,
Dropping from the clouds on high
Down into the sea beneath.
Death, death is in the slaty storm,
Whose latest volume vanisheth;
In the heart of its wild form
It rolls the fragment of my wreck :
The moon above it waits to die,
Waning to a ghostly speck
In the bloody morning sky,
Ghost of those who fled in death
And whose grave is underneath.
I am very lone.
The cold blue billows race along
These abject sands in ceaseless throng;
If the sun should rise to-day
They will be purple and scarlet grey :
I only feel alone.
If I did leap into the sea,
They would do the same to me.

Proserpine.

THE dragon earth with labyrinthine toils,
Terrace on terrace wound her stony coils,
And traversed towards a hollow deeply sunk,
With writhing stone-beds bordered : there had shrunk
Wide mouths that did volcanic flames embower
To blossom, as young spring's first yellow flower
Cleaves out its pathway through the blackened ridge ;
From this the white roads sped away to bridge
The bare lean-hearted hills ; and in their midst
Lo Demeter !   Sad goddess, wherefore didst
With thy small company of savage men,
Autochthonic, that night invade the den
Of dragon darkness and of nether light ?
For, lo ! the circling mists, grown infinite,
Do round themselves to many a torch and lamp ;
And with wild gleams of limbs, with rolling tramp,
With shoutings, pours thy pomp: it nears the spot
Where the deep earth-fires sleep awakened not.

High in her chariot rode the goddess, crowned
With golden harvest fruits that spread around
Her shoulder, and her silver sickle's gleam
Arched lucidly her forehead, that supreme
She rode; and now the wild diviner takes
The lustral lavers and the salted cakes;
And in the hollow, folded coil on coil,
Showing earth's roots encumbered with white spoil,—
Hollow enormous, holding murky light,
Giving for ever one side severed quite
From other by the fierce sheer intervals
Of duskiness, o'er which in sullen sprawls
The red flame casts itself to colour slime,
He sang—

Oh, prisoned where the earth doth climb
To upper air, in cavern halls,
Where flame-like wing and writhing limb
Whirl round thy throne, where thousand falls
Of Stygian waters eye thee cold,
Where the dull font of days outdoled
To mortal men drains dry and old,
Lethe's unaided brim.

Oh, throned beside the dragon black,
Who dies at his own mystery,
Being a god; oh, folded back
Where ghosts and larves do shriek and fly,

Where the four rivers of thy throne,
Phlegethon, Lethe, Styx, Acheron,
Cause earth's profaned womb to groan,
Echidna's brood to cry !

Lo ! here the blood of the black bull
Drips towards thee from thy mother's hearse;
Daughter of earth, be merciful
In Hades to our hopes and fears;
Art thou not orphaned on thy throne,
Far from the happy light that shone,
Far from thy ravished maiden zone,
Far from thy mother's tears !

In the Woods.

A STERNLY subtle horror grew within
The deep and shaggy wood; it seemed akin
To my sad thoughts; went on with scarce a turn
The timber pathway, till a sullen burn
Spread sideways like a white and whispering ghost,
So rippling into darkness and so lost.
Above the swamp the giant trees embrace
Like wrestling dragons, underneath the lace
Of their broad pennons; here a sullen bough
Short-lopped, gleams whitely, threatening through the
    sough
Of all the distant tree-tops, bids me cast
My weary expectation here at last.
I fall, I sink, beneath the leafy walls,
Which clash a little as the water falls
From bedded roots, and as the wistful wind
Once more bends back the trees : as if a blind
Sunbeam dashed yellow o'er the gloomy frond,
A strange decay is stealing over yond

Sycamore, touching half its leaves with green
Of sickly paleness, as I lie between
High springing grasses headed with small flowers.
The foxglove drops the bell the bee devours,
And lo ! a keener pang in my lost peace
Speaks meaningly ; the woodland terrors cease
As the wild bee from the deserted bell
Hums fiercely forth ; the stern clouds upward swell,
The ghostly water whispers now no more,
The twining trees are hidden on the shore,
As the light dies too ; rolling rank on rank,
The waves of darkness swallow up in blank
Submersion all things: then within my soul
Awoke a harmony that blent the whole
Of life—can death do more, shall death do less ?
O soul of my past life ! the bitterness
Of thy past pain hurts not the thing I am
In this deep hour; the senses cannot cram
The spirit with fresh food for memories;
No object now to eye or ear can rise,
And so the spirit settles into peace
Self-drawn, or drawn from Him who makes to cease
All trouble, and the inmost spirit bids
Consist in peace ; who nightly seals our lids
For this, and gives us timely hours like those,
When even the heart the spirit's calm o'erflows.
With whitest robes, whenever death shall come,
Shall both his hands be filled.　We travel home.

Love's Consolation.

BY THE MONK OF OSNEYFORD.

————◦◇◦————

THE thorn-tree keeps its leaves for ever green
All the year round; and when the wind blows keen,
And strips all trees the summer's pride and chief,
This holdeth fast, and will not quit one leaf.
Likewise when Christ had worn the thorny crown,
That year the sorry thorn-tree trickled down
With drops of blood, and ever since hath worn
Those bleeding berries in its leaves of thorn.
Wherefore all doleful lovers prize that tree,
Both for its sorrow and its constancy;
And all they say that it is good to wear
Its leaves so sharp and green upon their hair,
As Christ did then; for Christ who loved us died
In love of us, and whoso would abide
His baptism, must in loving die also,
That life may rise again from deathly woe.

6—2

It is great marvel to me that I keep
My hand in writing tales of love and sleep,
And life and God; for long ago has ceased
The stir of things in me; I stand released
A long time now from all that coil severe
Which knitteth heart to heart: I have grown clear
Perchance in watching our old Abbot's eyes,
Burn softly like a dove's, when he replies
To us who ask his blessing in the hall:
He gives the same old gift to great and small,
Just peering with his old mouth and white hair
At what you are, a moment; and, you swear,
As instantly forgetting: howsoe'er
The quiet of our life here day by day
Has somehow won on me to put away
All other thought save to write on and on,
Between the prayer times, as if life were gone
In threescore years for me as from the rest;
Alas! that earnest e'er should grow a jest!
    So let me reason how I first began
To write my tales in praise of those who ran
Furthest in love; of what did set me on
To make my body lean, and my face wan
In praising that which was my utter woe
A long time past: hear, and ye well shall know
That I fulfil my life in writing well
Of love and God, and life, the tales I tell.

It being then the happy Christmas time,
And all the orchards thick with frosty rime,
I took me by the happy paths that go
Along the dumb and frozen river, so
That I might taste the goodness of the day ;
Passing through many meadows on my way,
Where all the grass and flowers were dead asleep,
Through many sheepfolds full of bleating sheep,
By many watercourses, whereby grew
The little-headed willows, two and two,
And also poplars : onward thus I sped,
Until the pathway reached a little head
Of brushwood, screening up a wicket gate,
Whereat I entered, and beheld elate
A wide and scattered wood of late-leaved beech
And oaks and thorn-trees, standing on the reach
Of long-withdrawing glades : at sight of these
And the snow-dabbled grass, and broken knees
Of large red ferns in patches, as I went,
Felt I great exaltation and consent
Unto the sweetness of the place and day :
The robin called the merle, who was away,
And yet the robin answered from his bough :
The squirrel dropt from branch to branch, although
Few leaves did screen him ; and with frequent bounds
The rabbits visited each others' mounds,
And o'er the dead leaves pattered. Thus I went
Until I reached a little thorn-tree bent—

A thorn-tree knotted like a human throat,
Set so, and all its leaves together smote   `
Out the resemblance of a saddened face
Raised on two knotty arms, thrust, as for grace,
Among wild hair : the tree was such I saw,
And crossed the glades for, thinking with much awe
About the time of year ; for in seven days
Would be the shortest day ; and last year's haze
Rose all about me then ; last year that day
Found I that I was given all away
For nought ; and all that winter had I gone
In loneliness, and when the summer shone,
Sadder was I to see the buds drawn out
On the long branches till they tossed about
In perfect flower ; making me but more sad
To see the sweet completeness all things had.
And I remember, sleeping in my bed,
A mighty clap of thunder shook my head
About laburnum time ; and I awoke
And watched the lightning make a great white stroke
Three hours above the poplar tops, and then
Came morning and the writing of a pen
Telling me that my love and reverence
Three days before had sold herself for pence
Unto a clown who riches had in store ;
Yea, sold herself for that three days before.
Ah ! Lord, thy lightnings should have wakened me
Three nights before they did : more bitterly

Was nothing ever done; and all the moons
The golden apples ripened, came long swoons
Of utter woe and trouble, shot across
By roaring and sad weeping for my loss.
Nor found I quiet till the autumn time
Was finished, and brought back the frosty rime;
And knights rode forth to quest upon the leas,
And seek adventure underneath the keys
Of the bare ash-trees, and by wayside stones,
And where roads met; and then I thought my moans
Had been ill-spent, and half my pain was crime;
For while I was lamenting all the time,
I might have been at tennis, or have made
Six pictures, or twelve stories; so I said.

    Love hath great store of sweetness, and 'tis well;
A moment's heaven pays back an age of hell:
All who have loved, be sure of this from me,
That to have touched one little ripple free
Of golden hair, or held a little hand
Very long since, is better than to stand
Rolled up in vestures stiff with golden thread,
Upon a throne o'er many a bowing head
Of adulators; yea, and to have seen
Thy lady walking in a garden green,
Mid apple blossoms and green twisted boughs,
Along the golden gravel path, to house
Herself, where thou art watching far below,
Deep in thy bower impervious, even though

Thou never give her kisses after that,
Is sweeter than to never break the flat
Of thy soul's rising, like a river tide
That never foams; yea, if thy lady chide
Cruelly thy service, and indeed becomes
A wretch, whose false eyes haunt thee in all rooms,
'Tis better so, than never to have been
An hour in love; than never to have seen
Thine own heart's worthiness to shrink and shake,
Like silver quick, all for thy lady's sake,
Weighty with truth, with gentleness as bright.
  Moreover, let sad lovers take delight
In this, that time will bring at last their peace:
We watch great passions in their huge increase,
Until they fill our hearts, so that we say,
"Let go this, and I die;" yet nay and nay,
We find them leave us strangely quiet then,
When they must quit; one lion leaves the den,
Another enters; wherefore thus I cross
All lovers pale and starving with their loss.
  And yet, and yet, and yet, how long I tore
My heart, O love ! how long, O love ! before
I could endure to think of peace, and call
For remedy, from what time thou didst all
Shatter with one bad word, and bitter ruth
Didst mete me for my patience and my truth.
That way thou hadst: once, cutting like a knife,
Thy hand sheared off what seemed my very life,

And I felt outside coldness bite within :
The lumpish axe that scales away false skin
Of some corruption clumped upon the bark,
Leaves the tree aching with the pale round mark,
And sweating till the wound be overshot
By the gums swelling out into a blot,
Where the bees lose their wings, and dead leaves stick.
Even so, O love, my flesh was sore and quick
From that astonishment, when I seemed flayed,
Torn piecemeal up, and shred abroad, and made
A victim to some brutal lack of skill;
Yet kissing still the hand so rough to kill.
So, so; I never meant but to live on
The old, old way; now the old life is gone—
Has it ?—and left me living ! This I thought,
Kneeling before the thorn-bush, over fraught
With many memories, when I saw the sweet
Red berries hanging in it, and its feet
Rolled up in withered moss; also I saw
Birds sit among its sharp green leaves and caw.
Gently I drew a branch of berries down,
And severed it to be my very own,
And on a pine log, lying full hard by,
Cast I myself and looked upon the sky.
   Oh, then behold a glorious vision fair,
Which came to comfort me in that despair ;
Branched in the clouds I saw a mighty tree,
As dearly twisted as the thorn, as free,

As kindly wild, clear springing through the green
Fields of the frosty Orient, and between
Four great hills rooted, where the earth upreared
Herself into the sky ; and as this cleared
I looked towards the thorn-tree standing there,
So happy, with the woods about all bare,
And then nine gentle forms did I behold—
Five men and four sweet ladies, as I told—
All walking towards me, with a gentle pace,
Round from the thorn, all with full solemn face,
And head bent solemnly : to me they came,
One led the band, the rest led each his dame.

The first who came waved forth a long green wand,
Whereat the others in fair show did stand
Divided, four on either side, a knight
And queen together, on the left and right.
Those knights had golden crowns upon their heads,
And their long hair drawn out with golden threads,
And rightly were they harnessed, and each bore
A coronal of thorn leaves, with good store
Of berries red, which shone like drops of wine
Amongst the green leaves and the gold wire fine.
Those four queens wore the thorn-leaves ; I saw there
Red berries spread about upon their hair :
Their crisped tresses hung more clear and fine
Than yellow amber holding gold-red wine ;
Their looks were wildly gentle, and more fair
Than full-eyed fawn just shaken from her lair ;

Wild looks of sorrow, wildly worn and past;
Wild looks of wild peace, wildly won at last:
One wore a white robe, like a thin white cloud,
Through which strange drops of crimson slowly ploughed;
One wore a white robe with a crimson seam,
In which strange quivering shapes did hang and gleam;
One wore a robe of dark deep violet,
In which, like eyes, gold passion-flowers were set;
One wore a robe of saffron, shot and stained
With willow leaves, and wolfsbane purple-veined:
Each stood contented, with a tender white
Hand in the reverent holding of a knight.
    At sight of this fair worship I had dropped
Upon my knees, and then uprose and stopped,
Until they stood more near, and then again
Knelt down before them, being very fain
To gaze upon their glory all so nigh.
Then he who led them, with a bitter sigh,
Began to chide me gently for my fault
In leaving love, and making that revolt
From him, since not a man shall miss reward
From love, who pays true service and regard.
" Ah, sir," said I, " how in God's truth and mine,
How I have loved, never canst thou divine.
If I blame love I do not scorn his might,
And have no other done in love than right.
Nay, I so truly dealt with my false dame,
And spent such pains, that many cried her shame

Because she paid me nought for my long quest.
I hold that love lights love in gentle breast;
Now hath she left me nought but scorn and loss.
Oh, never meet with love ; oh, never cross
A fair false face to torture all your thoughts,
For ever brooding, fiend-like, on the thwarts
Of all the paths you move in ; better far
To wage with fortune such a cruel war
As makes all joy to be a sin and crime :
Oh, to live rankly were a blessed time
In such a beggar's filth and press of wants
As gives no leave for wasting royal grants
Of love upon some brainless beauty-snare,
As sweet as false : so he is sure to fare,
Who trusts a woman,—save the worship sweet
Of these dear ladies, who with pity meet
My cursed complaining : can I not suppress
Some bitterness of soul, this tide and stress?"
　　" Thou shalt not need," replied his sovereign voice ;
" Behold how they with pity droop in poise
Of their sweet heads ; for drop by drop thy rain
Has filled their cups, until they stoop and drain
Upon the ground their fulness—thy bestowing;
Then rise,—unemptied, but no more o'erflowing.
Ah ! lilies, ah ! sweet friends, weep not so sore ;
He who can rail in love hath yet good store
Of lightness left him, whensoe'er he take
Good counsel, good advisement, and awake

Unto himself, see what he hath, let pass
This frenzy, this lewd mist blown on the glass
Wherein his clear eyes should behold themselves.
Now take this counsel from me: wise man delves
In his own heart for comforts ; never seeks
Outside himself ; and falls not when fate wreaks
Herself on what he hath, but cannot smutch
That which he is : he hath his creed ; not much
To say, but cons it shortly, and so holds :
Being forearmed, 'tis drawing fast the folds
Of mail that hung unrivetted for air.
Hast not thou such a creed ? thou hast ? prepare
To hear me con it to thee, lest thou cause
Ladies weep for thee ; nay, shouldst make a pause
In nature's kindness for thee, and go mad,
And swash about in madness, thinly clad,
A violent creature sinning.   Think this o'er :
Wouldst in a vase of many crannies pour
And say the liquor should not flow throughout,
But keep in certain hollows ?   Have no doubt
Up to its level it will flood the whole :
So does the tide of love o'erflood the soul
Admitting it, and so to dumbness fill
With very fulness ; thou canst not distil
Into the air one sound not muffled up
In love; as after being filled, the cup
Gives not its crystal echo to the stroke
The same as empty : now in furious smoke

Thy love hath whirled itself away, and left
The vessel of thy nature all bereft
And emptied quite : now therefore it is due,
That it ring out its ancient tone as true
As at the first, ring loud and merrily,
Singing of old things in the time gone by,
Most precious to thy heart, recalling all,
With little pain for what is past recall."

     " O gentle ladies ! I have worship done,"
I answered, " even when I made my moan ;
O knights ! I long had known your name and state,
Had not this lay prevented, with debate
Of my st tnis : now tell me who ye be,
Which I in part already seem to see."

     " Nine lovers are we, who have lost our loves,
Alike we are in that, and us behoves
To hold together, for by unhappiness,
Not by our fault, we fell beneath the press
Of the monster time, that ever coils about
The universe, and beats life in and out,
Being one living flail, and quick and fierce,
And full of hideous fancies : sometimes steers
His bulk straight onwards to the flying life,
With blood-fret head produced before the grife
Wave of his monster trunk, as shoots a spar
Of some wave-wallowing wreck before the far
Rush of the savage tides that urge it on ;
Sometimes o'ertakes his prey, and straight is gone

In one quick flash of serpent head, and tongue,
And eyes, and then surrounds, and lashes strong
His sinewy tail before the victim's eyes,
In hideous gambols ; all the while snake-wise,
His head is japing close behind. Now we
Were played with thus : Jules there, who secretly
Torments the hand of Ellen till he grow
To feel a need of her, enough to know
That no one can replace his need of needs;
And Ellen, knowing well that still she feeds
With her own heart a fire that Jules can ne'er
Become the food for ; Mark, who in despair
Long ago calm holds only by the cross
Upon his sword, and thinks not of his loss,
Save joined with all that God must be ; Lucrece,
Whose eyes now gain beginnings of great peace,
Watching her thin hands and the flowers they hold ;
Gilbert, who stands half ruffled, feeling bold
To say and do what he would never do
Were the time come ; Madoline looking so
Having done great self-sacrifice in love,
Yet thinking rather of the cost than of
The joy that should be hers from nobleness;
Miles, whose eyes pale before the glorious dress
Of Columbe's hair, but she means nought for him,
Nor he indeed for her ; they scarcely dream.
All these are waiting ever—we all wait—
For some completion to fill up the date

Of life as yet unfinished ; yet I say,
Perhaps in vain, as thou too ; best are they
Who love their life in all things: is not life
Its own fulfilment ? Steadfast marble rife
With knotty veins, like thoughts, inscrutable,
Broods on the altar's frontel, takes the spell
Of every taper pure caressing it,
Of every sun that warms the shadow-fit
From its pale, tranquil, capable, cold face;
Lives under sun and shadow, lets light trace
Its crumbled grain, and darkness thicken on't,
Struck blind by neither, neither is its want.
Man should do more than marble ; make meet change
For day and night within himself, estrange
His heart from nought that meets him, even laugh
When bitter roots are given him to graff
Upon joy's stem, yea, even if it bear
Yew leaves and berries weighty on the air,
And dropping on the sleek soil underneath,
Where dead things rankle,—'tis a bloom from Death,
And true souls always are hilarious,
They see the way-marks on their exodus
From better unto better ; still they say,
Lo ! the new law, when old things pass away;
Still keep themselves well guarded, nothing swerve
From the great purposes to which they serve
Scarce knowingly ; still smile and take delight

In arduous things, as brave men when they fight
Take joy in feeling one another's might.
Ah! now, poor wounded man, drag not thy coils
In shattered volume sadly through the toils,
Backward and forward, tearing more and more
Each torn quick part, and adding to the sore
That earth-clods stick in, like a mangled worm.
There is one way for thee; but one; inform
Thyself of it; pursue it; one way each
Soul hath by which the infinite in reach
Lieth before him; seek and ye shall find:
To each the way is plain; that way the wind
Points all the trees along; that way run down
Loud singing streams; that way pour on and on
A thousand headlands with their cataracts
Of toppling flowers; that way the sun enacts
His travel, and the moon and all the stars
Soar; and the tides move towards it; nothing bars
A man who goes the way that he should go;
That which comes soonest is the thing to do.
Thousand light-shadows in the rippling sand
Joy the true soul; the waves along the strand
Whiten beyond his eyes; the trees tossed back
Show him the sky; or, heaped upon his track
In a black wave, wind-heaped, point onward still
His one, one way. O joy, joy, joy, to fill
The day with leagues! Go thy way, all things say,
Thou hast thy way to go, thou hast thy day

7

To live ; thou hast thy need of thee to make
In the hearts of others; do thy thing ; yes, slake
The world's great thirst for yet another man !
And be thou sure of this; no other can
Do for thee that appointed thee of God;
Not any light shall shine upon thy road
For other eyes ; and thou mayest not pursue
The track of other feet, although they drew
Lucidly o'er wide waters, like the dip
Of speeding paddles, like the diamond drip
Of a white wing upon a lake struck dead
With shadows; no, though the innumerous head
Of flowers should curtain up the foot that falls.
Thou shalt not follow; thee the angel calls,
As he calls others ; and thy life to thee
Is precious as the greatest's life can be
To him ; so live thy life, and go thy way.

  Now we have gained this knowledge by essay,
In part ; some struggling yet, for we all thought
To gain another, hand in hand, upcaught,
Drawn onwards our soul's path ; and of us some
About our hearts meshed the loved hair with comb
Of our great love, to twine and glisten there,
And when 'twas stiffened in our life blood dear,
Then was it rent away; (ah ! so with thee;)
We learn to pardon those who could not be
A part of us, their way lying different ;
And learn to waste no grief on our intent

Thus warped; but live on bravely; tend the sore
Just at odd moments, when it oozes gore
Less sufferably: how our eyes draw fire
From the fire fount of pain !   Our wounds grow
   drier,
And memories walk beside us, as a shade
Walks by a great magician in his trade,
When deep night falls on all the paths, and he
Discourses to his friend, invisibly
Accompanied ; our memories walk by us,
Stand by us, when we look on others thus,
Face upon face; steal from us half our thoughts,
Flake after flake ; us therefore it imports
To make them our good servants, as the mage
Uses his shadows upon service sage.
O faithful gobetweens ! knit each to each;
O memories ! give to dead lips living speech,
Limbs motion, eyes their spirit-pulse; bestow
On everything its value ; grow and glow
A white intensity of chastest flame,
That all things may but seem to make the same
Great undulation of a wave of heaven
That flowed to us; so giving and so given,
May we pass on to death !
                    Now, therefore, write
Tales of our true love; both of those who quite
Bootlessly thought that love unto their love
Must knit itself; and those who, happier, strove

Only with fortune, overcast at length
By death alone, and walking in the strength
Of meat long eaten in the desert since.
First act is over, and the next begins,
Yet proves the same again, for us and thee.
What next ?   Why, all is ended."
                                        " Plaudite
Remains," I cried, " though your five tragic acts
That should have been, are shortened: fate enacts
A two-act farce, the dream and the awaking."
" Farewell," said he, " give largely ; we are staking
A little on thy mercy.   Do thou write ;
Let thine eye soften o'er the page ; let spite,
And hate, and over-sadness die away ;
Thou shalt see others calming in the sway
Of all within them.   Love, too, blossoms out
More perfectly from agony and doubt ;
Hath wider ranges, and a kind of laugh
At human things in him ; in short, can quaff
Easier of joy ; can grasp the world and use ;
Is kindlier to all living life ; would lose
Not one process of nature ; but o'erspreads
In genial current all things ; hath no dreads,
No hates, no self-tormenting ; cherishes,
Blesses, and gives great teaching, for it frees :
Thus much more precious is love's after-birth."
Wind and much wintry blue then swept the earth.

Waiting.

———◇———

By the ancient sluice's gate
Here I wait, here I wait;
Here is the sluice with its cramped stone,
Which the shadows dance upon.
                    Here I wait.

Stone, with time-blots red and blue,
And white, the shadows tremble through,
When the sun strikes out through the poplars tall,
And the sun strikes out upon the wall.
                    Here I wait.

From the sluice the stream descends
A bowshot; then its running ends
In flags and marsh flowers; then it runs
Bright and broad beneath the suns.
                    Here I wait.

And to one side of it come down
The walls and roofs of our good town ;
The other side for miles away
The willows prick it short and grey.

Here I wait.

Any moment I might see
My lady in her majesty
Moving on from tree to tree
Where the river runs from me.

Here I wait.

Any moment she might rise
From the hedgerow, where my eyes
Wait for her without surprise,
While the first bat starts and flies.

Here I wait.

Here I lie along the trunk
That swings the heavy sluice-door sunk
In the water, which outstreams
In little runlets from its seams.

Here I wait.

The last yellowhammer flits,
The winds begin to shake by fits;
More coldly swing the mists and chase :
Thinking of my lady's face

Here I wait.

Like a tower so standeth she,
Built of solid ivory;
Her sad eyes well opened be,
Her wide hair runs darkly free.
                    Here I wait.

Her eyes are like to water-birds
On little rivers, and her words
As little as the lark, which girds
His wings to measure out his words.
                    Here I wait.

Here the crows come flying late—
One flies past me; past the gate
Of the old sluice another flies;
Heavily upwards they do rise.
                    Here I wait.

I am growing thoughtful now;
Will she never kiss my brow?
Solemnly I sit and feel
The edge upon my sword of steel.
                    Here I wait.

If she come, her feet will sound
Not at all upon the ground;
I think upon thy feet, my love,
Red as feet of any dove.
                    Here I wait.

Here my face is white and cold,
Here my empty arms I fold;
Here float down the beds of weeds,
With the fly that on them feeds.

       Here I wait.

A Nun's Story—Modern Rome.

---◦◦---

Before the great house on the Palatine
The blood as yet is purple on the vine,
Nor has it faded from the leather belt
On which 'twas poured when cursed Guido dealt
Last night his blow.   Ah, Guido ! down below
Lorenzo's grave they're digging by a row
Of broken wine-jars on the cellar shelf;
And there the snow-white body keeps itself;
And here above does Lady Catherine sit,
And watch the vine that points to her and it:
Two stories has the vine—her ear to please—
Two lovers walk beneath a cirque of trees
Which closes round a pool of water-lilies,
Whose bank so steep almost a little hill is;
And she will gather one of those white flowers—
No danger, yet his very spirit cowers
At thought of it for her ; upon his knees
He nerves himself, and holds her hand in his ;

Then forth they walk in bliss, but after them
A staggering shadow steals, a flashing gem
Curves through the dusky air,—Lorenzo falls,
Dyeing the grass; then to these cloistered halls
They drag her, force the habit o'er her head,
And leave her senseless on her novice bed.
These are the vine's two stories; just awake,
She hears them for the first time, scarcely quake
Her eyes, but gaze far, far beyond the hills
In meditation how the deep air fills
With sea-like purple all the hollow land.
Poor angel! quickly wilt thou understand,
Oft wilt thou hear them with a wild despair
Too awful, writhing, shuddering, sobbing there,—
Would thou couldst die; and yet, if souls can guess,
I think that o'er death's purple haziness
A great white cloud is floating, heavenly fair,
On which she sits, as purely white; her hair
Blessed with the rainbow, and her feet just dipped
In the dark flood beneath; and, lo! now slipped
From some high heaven his spirit headlong falls,
To clasp her round the neck; alas! it palls,
And the long years by moments 'gin to fly—
Alas! poor angel, would that thou couldst die!

A Monk's Story.

I SAW to-day a man upon his back
Beneath a tree, watching the sailing track
Of quails and pigeons in the smoke-blue sky ;
And as their wings dipt deeper or more high
Above the shining leaves, I knew the man
With dizzying eyes more thoughtfully would scan
The heaven's blue burning till he fell asleep,
For all the day the heavens with light grow deep.
I knew that if a bittern or a quail
With shortened wings and pouncing feet should sail
Down through the air and settle on the tree,
The man would sleep no more, but suddenly
Spring up and drag his bow-case from his head.
Behold me in the life I sometime led !
    I know not how I sinned : what man can know
All he has sinned ? but very long ago,
In the beginning of my bootless tale,
Found I myself weeping without avail,
As who begins to live, and with a sense
Of long, long love, now reaching prevalence.

One lay beside me on a little mound,
Marsh marigolds and river reeds were round,
And three hours ere the sunset, and not far
A river rippling over a sandbar;
Gleaming the spacious shallows of its tide,
As if the moving were a breeze inside;
The purple shadows trembling through and through,
Above, around us, who were trembling too.
Who lay beside me on the little mound?
My hands were beating on the harmless ground:
Weeping, why wept I in the golden air,
So passioned in the depths of what despair?
He, strange companion, heeded not at all;
Prostrate he lay, as he were past recall
For weariness; one knee was bent and raised,
And ever upwards at the blue he gazed
Where small white clouds went on. How bitter-sweet,
How bitter; but I will not use deceit,
I will not hide, nor tell how, after this
Long years, betrayed by a Judas kiss,
Sent me kiss-stung and madding through the world:
For who would curse? Have I found peace upcurled
In yond volumen I illuminate?
I will not bid my saint a moment wait,
Whilst I in his grim acts interpolate
A weaker man and unappointed fate.
So there's my monogram in silence put
Upon the page in which my life is—shut:

And when ye take my volume from the shelves,
And stare upon it while ye cross yourselves,
Think thus upon the painter, simple friends :—
He was a man at quiet war with fiends,
Ora pro animâ, he painted here :
This is a morn in spring ; how high uprear
To meet the blue our white-brown convent walls,
And from them a translucent shadow falls
O'er half the cell ; and what a diaper
The little leaves and branches all astir
With sunshine, pour upon the picture screen !
He painted here, happy he must have been ;
He was a good man and did visions see,
A quiet man without a history ;
Think thus, and pity me, and pray for me.

Ay, and this morn in spring, midst this design
To which I thought was given this life of mine,
Stirring the quiet sunshine of my cell,
Something across the blazoned parchment fell :
A shadow, not flung down from swinging bough,
I caught it ; 'twas the arching of a brow,
And gloss of purple hair was what I saw,
And stealing footsteps, which could not withdraw :
What ! she, that trembler whom one sees about
Our gates, who bows and tries to look devout ?
And he, our latest joined, whose flesh is weak ?
Well, sin no more; I am not one to speak.

Ballad.

LORD Robert and fair Ellen both
  Came flying on a horse of might :
They left five brethren on the ground
  Before they fled from hall that night.

The first river they came unto,
  It did but wet the horse's feet :
It was as sad as the ashes of fire ;
  Long time they tarried in its street.

"And oh ! fair Ellen," Lord Robert said,
  "I had slain but four instead of five !"
"Now rest thee well, Lord Robert," she said,
  "For thou and I are here alive."

The next river they came unto
  It went up to the horse's knees ;
The ice was broken all about ;
  It shone like the sun on the leaves of trees.

"And would for thy sake we both had died,
  Before I stood within thy bower!"
"I greeted thee well, Lord Robert," she said,
  "And better to think of the sweet than the sour."

The third river they came unto
  To the middle of the flank increased;
The ice was sailing all around,
  It shone like the sun on the fell of a beast.

"Ah! where is thy false nurse Jan this night,
  Who kept the watch above thy bower?"
"Nurse Jan needs watch no more," she said,
  "And better to think of seed than sower."

The next river they rode unto,
  Over the wither-band did break;
The ice did break on fair Ellen's foot,
  It shone like the sun on a coiling snake.

"We never have met, I swear to thee,
  Alas! and we are woe together."
"Have courage, my lord," fair Ellen said,
  "We two shall merrily win this weather."

The next river they came unto,
  The stream ran over the horse's flank;
The ice poured down from side to side,
  It shone like shore-grass dry and lank.

He never spake a word again,
  But drew her arm right through his own ; '
She bent her white hand in his hand,
  Until it pressed on his breast-bone.

The next river they came unto,
  It rose up to the horse's head ;
A fire upon the midst did burn,
  The waves like rolling meadows spread.

The ice rolled heavily about,
  Like briny monsters of the sea :
He drew her round him on the horse,
  And there they two well buried be.

113

La Faerie, or Lovers' World.

ARGUMENT.—Mark, while uncertain about his own destiny, sees La Faerie in a dream, and hears two of its inhabitants relate their story in conversation with one another. Their union had been opposed, the lover unwillingly slew a rival of whom he had no fears, and after three years killed himself, on a report of the lady's forced marriage. On his death the lady retired to a convent, and after nine years died.

I.

SAT Mark within the shadow of a gloom
Made by his banner hung against the sun,
Woven blue and green; beside him in the room
Another chair, whereon were made to run
Strange beasts, and on the top a white, white dove
   Strained always its spread wings towards that serene
   Heaven of the banner woven blue and green.

II.

At that time went the clouds from far above,
   Wind-grouped, to pause with golden ministries
About the sun; at that time no remove
   From very life were those hued images
And whelming sounds one has who dreams, yet wakes,
   Musing about the inmost core of things,
   The land of wonder and its splendorings.

8

III.

About high hills embowering endless lakes,
   About strange mariners on savage shores,
About sea-billows swelling with huge aches,
   About black murders done on secret moors,
About the panic dances in the night,
   About stern booming sounds in solitudes,
   And moon-made goblins seen in shuddering woods.

IV.

To Mark that sunset shaped its end aright,
   Coming to this, that in the chair by Mark
His lady sat, no later than last night,
   When they two sat together until dark,
He, kissing at her shadow in his heart,
   She, perfect in her hues; he, heart-elate;
   Both silent, like the love-bird and its mate.

V.

We nothing understand for our sad part
   How what has been, becomes what is to be :
We wake from cabin dreams with bodeful start
   And find ourselves at welter in the sea;
So miserable, prayer might feel afraid
   Of God, except that ever Fancy leaves
   Some slippery trail of joy while she deceives.

VI.

Now on Mark's eyes a husky shadow preyed,
  In which his eyeballs smouldered black and fierce ;
And presently he bit his banner's braid,
  Straining it tighter lest some glint should pierce
And make less holy that which was his thought :
  He would as soon have spoken of his dreams
  As opened them to unabated beams.

VII.

So onward fares in dreams till he is brought
  To life and death, in summit of them both ;
Tottering upon half thoughts, pale, scarcely raught,
  Clinging upon him, frantical to clothe
Their thinness in the shadow substances
  In which his soul was ravelled, tissue-wise,—
  Live memories, sweetest thoughts, and glad surprise.

VIII.

Now hither, moonbeams, in your essences
  Fading from night, ere night herself can close :
Now Boreals, splintered on ice palaces
  In twenty sunsets and a million glows ;
Now hither all sweet lights and ravishments
  Of colour, primes, and germs, and slow decays,
  And stealing time-marks, and uncertain sways.

IX.

And vast and mighty overfalls and rents
　In tawny clouds, through which the pale sun shows
A revelation—give me sacraments
　Of poetry to swear on ; for by those,
And other such-like mighty mysteries
　Dream-born, dream-nursed, my lady's life hath grown
　To be the marvel we shall gaze upon.

X.

Whence cometh she ? for sure again his eyes
　Are fed on her, the chair again enfolds
His love, his sweetest; yet he scarce descries
　His lady in the shadow he beholds ;
His lady there, not perfect in her hues,
　Too pale for her ; but ere his passion speaks,
　The crimson, flagging slowly to her cheeks,

XI.

There fluctuates in tongues of flame that use
　Their splendours on the heart's weak blood to feed :
Back, forward, backward ; utterly suffuse
　The heavenly places where it is their need ;
And now the circles of sweet violet
　Are traced beneath her mystical blue eyes:
　Oh, let her lift them ere her lover dies !

XII.

My lady lives in perfect glory set,
　My lady lives all perfect in her hues,
And is yon orb La Faérie, which doth fret
　With little glints the stillness which doth muse,
And lightens vainly on her presence meek
　Yet mighty in its saddened majesty,—
　A statue always heaving with a sigh !

XIII.

Herewith that lover felt his passion speak,
　Beginning, " An angel out of paradise,"
Yet marks her lips apart ere he can wreak
　The pains within him on the ecstacies;
And she is shaken through her presence sweet,
　Yet on he breaks impetuous : " Rosalys ! "
　(First to pronounce that music be it his),

XIV.

" O love ! O love ! O sweet ! let me but meet
　Thy hand in mine, and we shall be the thing
That poets sing of in their highest heat,
　And, therefore, more than poets, journeying—
Oh ! thus and thus ; I bless thee, thus and thus :
　I'll bear thee, dearest, tenderly alive,
　Where'er yon orb of swiftness shall arrive.

XV.

"For see, it grew most largely over us,
    Put forth two wings, and glowed with presences,
Shaking with spangles, thronged, tumultuous,
    With happy faces, like the waves of seas,
Still changing as it moved, and one serene
    Bright ray of redness touched upon thy face,
    Then vanished starlike, with a final trace

XVI.

"Of blue that glided swiftly into green;
    It is La Faërie, that happy place ;
And all those happy faces we have seen
    Are lovers proved and worthy of their grace.
I take this token for our summoning ;
    Wherefore, O love, 'tis now to flee away,
    Leaving the dead world and the dying day."

XVII.

This passion was a dream, I think, to cling
    About the heart, and never come to deed ;
There are some passions which do only ring
    An inward voice, and inly are decreed ;
This passion faded quickly, being spent
    Before the coming on of words wherein
    Its argentine completedness to win.

XVIII.

But this no dream, that ever as he leant
  Full-browed towards her, swift as is the flight
Of white doves from some resting eminent
  Towards the green beneath, where they alight
After one cleaving of the air with wings,
  Two lovers, as they seemed, together sped
  Down through the still air in the twilight spread,

XIX.

Coming as from La Faërie, which with rings
  Of amethyst darker belting its thick blues
And hinted greens, across heaven's quarterings,
  Beyond the sunset pours its bickering hues,
Like runes, and fuses all things to the point,
  Where all things seem to keep good company,
  And yet may change, nor lose one just degree.

XX.

Those lovers twain, be very sure, did join 't,
  That fellowship of beauty, and they sat
In front of all its harmonies; Aroynt,
  You could not say at such a time as that
To any evil thing, for there was nought
  But seemed at one with all things, no surprise
  In that vast scape of mingled forms and dyes.

XXI.

Presently ran a thread of talk inwrought
    Into the silence, which was musical,
From those paired lips, rich-purpled, overfraught
    With kisses, hanging only till the fall
Of converse : then she answered unto him :—
    " All that long time they were tormenting me,
    My lips formed silently the name of thee.

XXII.

" Those three with their pressed brows curved, and the rim
    Of their long eyes settled in watchful scorn;
And he, who could not, like them, always dim
    His fury in the cruel system, worn
By them, of scorn, which masked a killing rage ;
    Sisters and father : spite of scorn and blame,
    My lips were curving ever with thy name.

XXIII.

" And so I kept me, looking not on age
    Defaced with fury, nor on that tiger-like
Contempt crouched ring on ring ! a weary stage
    Of life it was;—one watching how to strike,
One silent in prevention ; once alone
    Did they surprise me.   Shall I tell you it,
    That triumph of those cruel women's wit ?

XXIV.

" My strife was at its height a day, when one
   Of them came pitying to me, that she knew
And sorrowed for my heart; her softened tone
   Touched me as the baked earth is touched by dew;
Wherefore I loosened from my hold on calm,
   Suddenly fluttered in half joy, half shame,
   And broke my heart in uttering out thy name.

XXV.

" Whereat they laughed from ambush, and her palm
   Smote me to redness on my cheek ; for me,
I wept along, regardless, on my arm,
   Amidst the laughter of the cruel three."
" O love, O suffering love !" Can I rehearse
   How they two kissed in memory of her wrong ?
   Then took she up her sequel like a song.

XXVI.

" Until the old man leaped out with a curse,
   To see me in my constant weeping there,
Making confession, bearing all his worse,
   Because my better gave me grace to spare;
So drove me home in my still place to yearn."
   He.—" We met." *She.*—" Yes, yes." *He.*—" Ah,
     after that you gave
   Dear prayers to me to pity and to save.

XXVII.

" Yet after wouldst not, dearest, in my turn,
  Though I prayed, lover-like, with eye and lip;
I chill, I chill; thou wouldst not, wouldst not learn
  My plan ; so let that indignation slip,
Which should have wrought deliverance. Oh, thou sweet,
  Why wouldst not listen ?   Almost am I grieving
  To think of all that gladness of our leaving."

XXVIII.

She.—" And yet sometimes it happened us to meet,
  And sure the sudden rapture of a look,
On which we lived whole days in thought, complete
  In filling up what should have been, partook
Of ecstasy, threefold of ecstasy."
  He.—" O me ! you know not, love, how terrible
  To see thy heaven ; then writhe alone in hell.

XXIX.

" For you, as women can, went tranquilly
  Among them all ; I knew not how you beat
To fold me closely, as I beat for thee;
  You left me always maddening in my heat."
She.—" Well, well, sometimes we met." *He.*—" Yes,
    yes, we met;
  Once when the olives, like blue smoke, were faint,
  I saw you coming towards me, like a saint.

XXX.

" How you were there, I there, I know not ; let
   This knowledge serve ; how anguishing we clung
On one another ; 'twas something, that." *She.*—Ah ! fret
   No more ; bethink thee of that time you swung
Up to my window, and that pale, pale lad
   Watching you in and out ; and never spoke,
   Nor crossed your path, but looked as if he woke.

XXXI.

" What joy had he compared with what you had;
   He, looking for my eyes the whole day long,
He, sickening for my hands." *He.*—" It makes me mad."
   She.—" He ne'er had aught from me—could I belong
To two at once ? he cast himself away
   On me and thee." *He.*—" It makes me very sad
   To think of all the bitterness he had."

XXXII.

She.—" Poor face, poor face ! Yes, still I see the glow
   On his lithe lips whenever I came near ;
Give love for love, at last he said ; and No
   I answered, but I stroked his long lank hair,
And that was well." *He.*—" 'Twas well." *She.*—" And
     then my sire
Cut me with querulous curses, and the three
   Sprang from their tiger-lair, and tore at me.

XXXIII.

" Had they not so, 1 know not but the wire
　Of pity had been strung to love for him :
Therefore we do not blame them." *He.*—" No, suspire
　With pity for that phantom grey and grim;
Once was our meeting in the narrow street,
　Thy sire chafed fiercely, palsying with his sword
　At mules and servants, as became a lord.

XXXIV.

" You, gold and velvet falling to your feet,
　You, golden cinctures floating round your head ;
And still the crowd drove us together, sweet,
　I saw but you amid the hustling tread
Of those sworn servitors and their fierce chief,
　Who thrust right furiously against my breast,
　And clutched upon and tore aside my vest.

XXXV.

" Were the three with you then ?" *She.*—"Another grief
　We had, that sometimes if we heard a bell,
Or all things shook together in change, or if
　Some splendour just seen vanished as it fell
From heaven with sweet superb upon the green,
　We saw, and saw not, sickened, all in vain,
　We cried aloud, as children cry in pain."

XXXVI.

He.—" Yes; one time in the church, I think you mean.
   In my sick longing for your face I watched
How one sat always reading in the screen
   A book of saints where gold and crimson matched ;
And lo! you came, yet came not: shadow-shade
   Darkened upon the windows, and a trance
   Baffled me for a moment in its dance.

XXXVII.

" Like to a blind man holding out his head
   To solemn night, one sat within the porch,
Who starting at some noise which had been made,
   At that time, I remember, in the church,
Turned slowly his look inwards with his eyes
   Full, yet of dreamlight, oh ! so weird and wan,
   Still musing of the thing he dreamed upon.

XXXVIII.

" I would have passed, knowing him, but sighs,
   Which either breathed, made pause between us twain,
We looked at one another; his surprise
   Grew full within him ; but the sense of pain
Steadied him, and his words came hot and fast—
   ' Thou canst not love, thou dost not love, as I,
   I seek for death, the one of us shall die ! '

XXXIX.

" Well, I was sad; and yet I would have passed;
  And yet my sword was out; his sword swung thick
Hissing about my head; I struck at last,
  And felt my sword slide instant to the quick,
Then drag through bitten flesh, all wet and cold ;
  His blood spun out and burst against the wall ;
  I listened afterwards to hear it fall.

XL.

" Thence thrice had new things swallowed up the old,
  Thrice had the summer boughs drooped down with song,
Three summers had consumed spring's manifold
  Incenses in their fervid censers hung,
And it was now the autumn yellow-haired,
  When died I for thy love; for they had said
  Three years before that you perforce were wed.

XLI.

" Three years I saw you never, yet I spared
  To slay myself, and then it was enough ;
I ne'er should see you, and no longer cared;
  Joyfully died I, thus I gave rebuff
To the foul lie that ankered in my brain,
  That love was dead within me, for I knew
  'Twas still in me that love should pierce me through.

XLII.

" Even as of old when thrilled I with sweet pain
  Of love, but now the old love, overborne
By faces new and those long years, seemed fain
  To lurk in secret places and to mourn
Its potence lost; and yet I knew full well
  That it was there, and might revive at once,
  If anything should touch it for the nonce,

XLIII.

" If any breath should breathe that ancient spell,
  If any look 'should give thy face recall;
But still the occasion came not which should quell
  The unmeaning present, and 'twas natural
That I should die, for such a life was death,—
  That I should let my sluggish soul have scope
  To find despair, since it abandoned hope.

XLIV.

" Oh! one might live in anguish, and draw breath
  Of liquid flame, unshrinking ; but to feel
The heart freeze harder, while o'erflourisheth
  The life of sense, and that to uncongeal,
Awaits the blindness of some accident,
  This is the death indeed. Ah! who would wend
  Through years of lifeless life to such an end ?"

XLV.

She.—" But *thrice* three years were counted in event
  Of patience strong in its grave monotone;
Nine solemn years fell over, ere *I* leant
  To give deliverance to my soul outgrown;
Nine years the sunbeams saddened into night,
    Nine years the moonbeams tasted my sad cheek,
    Nine years the visions left me wan and weak.

XLVI.

" What, you were dead? I died too, and outright
  I buried me, where might I evermore
See visionary change of shadow-light
  Steal through my prison, telling o'er and o'er
The crevices and hues of grey-cold stone,
    That anguish might be dulled by watching so,
    And slowly, slower, cease my pulses slow.

XLVII.

" And if at any time some vision lone
  Should shape towards me, it might solemner
Pass over that cold mirror, and be gone
  Without surprise, joining the wistful stir
Of gentle death within me; mystical
    I watched the moon-forms in the unstirred nights,
    Trembling upon each other with delights

XLVIII.

" Which touched me to the core, and drew the fall
  Of tears, soon checked, one flutter and its pause;
Dear heart, I cried for thee whene'er the pall
  Drawn from my heart gave me such sudden cause;
A dread time was the day, severe and dull,
  Ministering of nought, but with the night came hot
Reflections from the life which now was not.

XLIX.

" Wherefore I wandered forth by night, brimful
  Of fiery thought, which ever overbrimmed
Like a fire-fountain in its rise and lull,
  Dewing the fair locks of the vapour-dimmed
White-raimented sweet saints who bosomed round;
  I sought the wild path of the soaring moon,
My star, my fate, who gave me all that boon.

L.

" But when she levelled with the horizon's mound
  Her speckled mirror, speeding fast away,
Then every spot and tuft upon the ground,
  Rounded with shadow, domed and coned, and gray,
And shaking with the secrets of the wind,
  Circled my feet so lovingly, and made
Their signs to me, that I no farther strayed;

9

LI.

Until the lion colour, which had skinned
 The nether clouds, had left them black and vast
In the moon's setting ; then too paled and thinned
 The unshaped purpose which had bound me fast;
And all was withered, dark, and gray again;
 Except that sadness, ere she took her place,
 Granted me to bemoan my minished space."

LII.

"' Then,' cried I out, impatient in my pain,
 ' Earth has her need of heaven, to order right
The many wrongs of which she bears the stain:
 O God ! O God of heaven ! again 'tis night,
Now all things wear their weird and pallid look;
 I wait for something which will never come;
 Let the heavens answer; be no longer dumb

LIII.

" It was as when one gazes on a book;
 Those agonies foredoomed, like weary thought,
Came with the power of ravishment, and took
 The passive nature, which resisted nought,
Caught it, and bore it onwards, and anon
 Let fall, let sink, upon the former state
 Of intense apathy completing fate.

LIV.

" Now those nine years had all my bloom foredone,
  And sapped my form, and left me stooped and wan.
When those nine years at length upon me shone,
  Flashed out the strange road I had journeyed on,
And towards the end I wondered what the end
  Would be, astonished at that period
  Of mad self-torture, the forgotten God

LV.

" By silence making for Himself amends
  Upon my silence: ' God,' I shrieked aloud,
' My life, my life ! oh, give me life to spend,
  Give back the life I've murdered in the cloud ! '
This was my waking; with wild eyes I saw
  Before me nothing, not one step to take:
  Ah ! best have prayed, still sleeping, not to wake !

LVI.

" No voices anywhere, which is the law ;
  No answer, save the silence of the heaven ;
No consolation, save the awe in awe;
  No hope, save portion with the unforgiven ;
No love, for thy dear image in that hour
  Seemed loosened from my heart; I groaned, and said,
  ' Where art thou, love, now that I am dismayed ? '

LVII.

" But in that winter time I marked the tower
    Of ashen light—the snow had clad the pine
Upon the mountain—how the glens did pour
    Like cataracts downwards towards the gorged ravine,
Leap after leap, snow-shadow and snow-light,
    And steppe on steppe; and upwards, pine on pine,
    The snowy mountain rose up crystalline.

LVIII.

" And panic-struck I watched the changeful height
    Until the sunset mocked me with its rose,
Until that rose was blenched in utter night,
    And all was gray and barren on the snows.
I lay upon a little mound below,
    I ceased not gazing on the darkened line
    Where heaven o'erhung the mountain palatine.

LIX.

" And then outwent there, like a whisper's flow,
    A little stir of light about the sky ;
The mountain's head came out by touches slow,
    And the moon took her clouds, and wrought thereby
A vision's bed, and presently she came,
    My star, my fate, all hurried to my sight,
    And on my weak sense burst the Infinite.

LX.

" Oh, I was lapped in gold, and dipped in flame,
Those billowy-bosomed clouds were all aglow
With presences, and I beheld the same,
Those ministrants came crowding row on row,
And in their sovereignties thy face was plain ;
Flame hands and voices calling me away—
I gathered up my soul and left the clay."

LXI.

Who hath despaired let him despair again ;
What hath been shall be, and our very life
Is reproduction ; pleasure's shadow, pain ;
Earth's destiny, to live and die in strife ;
Man's reason, but the tracer of God's will,
A faint and scarcely faithful shadow thrown
From the all-Reason who abides alone.

LXII.

God's reason,—Let alone this evil still ;
Let heaven still stand above the earth, apart,
As though the heaven were brass, inflexible,
As though the earth were not the heaven's heart.
Mark rose as if from dreams, and sadly prayed,
With night's thick darkness poured upon his head ;
Of him I saw no more : consider this,
How long ago died Mark and Rosalys.

Mother and Daughter.

HEAR now, my daughter, what I say;
I came into that house one day,
The twisting apple-trees were bloom,
I sat a long time in that room;
The house rose just above the stream
Upon the bottom of a seam
Of hill that rises high beyond,
All bare except the little bond
Of apple-yard enclosed behind
The house, and all so steep inclined,
The highest apple-tree appeared
One level with the gable reared ;
And need had I to think, I ween,
The twinkling flax was living green.
With fleecy moss and misletoe
Those trees will now be gray, I know ;
But then they had a wondrous glow,
Their roots were in the earth below,
Their blossom in the heaven above.
The blue wind rose and gently clove

The pearl-green leafage from the glume,
And bore it to the brook to bloom ;
And need had I to think, I ween,
About your gold hair's glorious sheen,
Yet not so fair as mine had been ;
And your eye living in the noon
Of life, yet singing no such tune
Of life, I thought, as mine did once ;
Of thee, sweet virgin, for the nonce
Unbroken in thy heart, my maid,
My virgin, from my bowels flayed.
Of thy sweet peace as yet unpained,
Of thy sweet mercy yet unstained,
Of thy sweet angel yet unfrayed,
Of thy sweet service, to be paid,
Of thy sweet humour, not yet dim,
Of thy sweet blessings made for him ;
'Twere need, I ween, to think of these
Beneath the apple-trees.
    His spirit there before me stood,
It dropped out of the apple wood,
It went before me where I sat,
Through the house and past the cat,
It passed the brook, it passed the road,
But led me towards our old abode ;
And at the turnstile turned, and saw
Me following, then took its law

Of vanishing from mortal sight ;
I kept that way with steady might,
And came upon you both, and found
What 1 had wished—his arms around
Your golden head, while muttering burned
His lips upon your lips upturned.
He's dead, and I am forty year ;
You are a mother now, my dear.

The Groomsman.

HER bridal feast is fairly set,
  She smiles with innocence and joy,
She smiles into her bridegroom's heart,
  Innocent girl and happy boy.
    What pity can she have for me?

Why am I here to walk behind,
  And hold his handkerchief or glove;
The vow which gives him heart and life
  To me but gives a sister's love.
    What pity can she have for me?

All that a man can do is done;
  I met her in the cedar wood:
To all that I could say or pray
  Her sorrow wept, her purpose stood:
    What pity can she have for me?

And now she smiles : ah ! happiness,
Thou cruel child, thou bitter joy :
She knows not if my heart be rent :
Innocent girl and happy boy.
What pity can she have for me ?

Despair.

I FIND myself by a black spring and cold,
  Which slowly bursts from this rock's heavy head,
Like drops of sweat wrung from our God of old,
      And plashes dead
Into a basin hollowed from the mould.

I trace this fountain rolling deeply down—
  Dark is the night, my pathway ruinous—
Here foam the muddy billows thick and brown,
      Then issue thus
Into a lake where all the world might drown.

I mark the mountains stand about and brood—
  The lake and they together, God, remain,
As black and deep and steep as walls of mud
      On some vast plain
Block out and brood upon a swimming drain.

I mark a woman on the farther shore
　Walk ghost-like ; her I shriek to with my might;
Ghostlike she walketh ever more and more ;
　　　Her face how white !
How small between us seems the Infinite !

I call her, but she ever tacks and veers
　Like some wan sail that sails in the salt seas
Unheeding all the shore's strained eyes and ears;
　　　Must this not cease ?
Ah ! hear my cry, dear soul, and give me peace.

I call her ; never may she heed or note :
　Is this the end ?　Just Judge, this place is cursed!
Each breath I draw within my beating throat
　　　Doth make and burst
Bubbles of blood.　Death, death !　Death last and first.

Sonnet.

GIVE me the darkest corner of a cloud,
  Placed high upon some lonely mountain's head,
Craggy and harsh with ruin ; let me shroud
  My life in horror, for 1 wish me dead.
No gentle lowland known and loved of old,
  Lure me to life back through the gate of tears ;
But long time drenched with rain and numb with cold,
  May I forget the solace of the years:
No trees by streams, no light and warmth of day,
  No white clouds pausing o'er the happy town ;
But wind and rain, and fogbanks slow and gray,
  And stony wastes, and uplands scalped and brown ;
No life, but only death in life: a grave
As cold and bleak as thine, dear soul, 1 crave.

The Crusader's Monument.

HANDS at rest
Cross my breast,
Left arm closes sword to side;
Thus I slept
When we leapt
From the saddle at eventide.

Like a tent,
My monument
Soars o'er me to its height of arch;
My burgonet
Is rivelled yet,
As if against the morrow's march.

Morning's beam
Strikes a gleam
From my shield hung up on high:
Had a foe
Struck that blow,
Should I start to arms and issue try?

Here the rood
Years hath stood,
As it shook over me in the clanging strife ;
  Ah! poor knight,
  Thou dost fight
For holy cross another life.

Work was mine
In Palestine,
When the Paynims howled round me as I lay;
  Here they pray
  Night and day,
But I fight with long fiends since my dying day.

Romance.

Look you be sure,
Take here the lure;
Ride you there, ride you for one two and three.
Down the king's fist
With the drag of the wrist,
Dragged down the pomegranates pierced with the bee.

There he sits thinking,
Stolid and blinking,
While the recorder doth read the decree;
Courtiers unto him
Talk the thing, view him;
There he sits gartered well under the knee.

Rightly be swift,
Lightly let lift
Bridle, and ride to the tower of the sea;
On the queen's face
Sorrow to trace
Seeds of the pomegranate sanguine and free.

There she lies faintly,
On her breast quaintly
Lies her plumed peacock fan ; dead she may be :
With her together
One loosened feather
Waves near her mouth: she has drawn up her knee.

On to your courser,
Spare not his horsehair ;
Ride to the knight of the tower of the sea ;
Long ago bade he
Carry my lady
Into his tower ; carry her, carry me.

There he sits waiting,
Counting and rating
Sunflowers that grow by his wall on the lea:
Sees the long grasses,
Browsed on by asses,
While he makes songs with his harp on his knee.

Now he is gone ;
Cross-bolt or stone
Swiftlier fled never, think I, than he:
Hark how the feet
Lessen their beat:
Four dies to two ; so there, give me the key.

10

There he emerges
Close where the verge is;
Now he is shot past our furthest off tree:
Grant he come back,
(Riding not slack,)
I, maiden Alice, will stand at his knee.

The Judgment of the May.

Come to the judgment, golden threads
   Upon golden hair in rich array;
Many a chesnut shakes its heads,
   Many a lupine at this day,
Many a white rose in our beds
   Waits the judgment of the May.

Oh, like white roses, great white queen,
   Come to the judgment, come to-day.
The white stars on thy robes of green
   Are like white roses on trees in May:
By me thy stars and flowers are seen,
   But now thou seemest far away.

Song.

———◦◦◦———

BRIGHTLY glance the beech-tree tops,
  The aspen quivers bright;
The poplar swings from out the copse
  And lashes into white.

Brightly glance the clover tops,
  The hedge-rows glisten sweet,
Where freely climb the flowering hops,
  And bells and flower-buds meet.

Brightly glance the willow heads,
  The stream comes gleaming down and raving;
Beside it wave the osier beds,
  But love is more than all their waving.

Brightly glance the tops of the oaks,
  The branch of the ash is black and bitter;
Round the sun's blue course the fire-cloud smokes,
  To me earth's darkness were dearer and fitter.

Brightly glance the tops of the broom,
  Bright swells the thicket's side;
The clustering branches give no room:
  Oh, where may love abide !

A Song of Three Maidens.

OF maidens three but one I knew,
I dream about the other two :
Sometimes I dream and then I see
    My maidens three.

When white primrose at last begin'th
To yield to wild blue hyacinth,
Then does the vision come to me
    Of maidens three.

When apple blossom falls away,
And lilies feel the first decay,
Then shall the vision finished be
    Of maidens three.

To Shadow.

If ever thou didst creep
From out the world of sleep,
When the sun slips and the moon dips,
If ever thou wast born ;
Or upon the starving lips
Of the gray uncoloured morn.

If ever thou didst fly
In the darkness of the sky,
When it was shaded and cloud-invaded,
And thou didst form and flit
By the wild wind aided,
Like a phantom shed from it.

If ever thou didst fall
Less and less upon the wall,
When the noon heat gathered and beat;
And if thou didst grow amain
To thy former size complete,
As the hours increased again.

If ever thou didst hover
Large and larger, till thy cover
Hid all things hence from the world's sense,
So that we said no more
(In thy total prevalence)
Art thou here as before.

If ever thou wast broken
By the moon which gave her token,
When she broke thee, that she woke thee,
And restored thee to our sight
By the many rays which stroke thee
Of her interfluent light.

If ever thou didst pass
Into blue along the grass,
And into blue the long wood through,
When the sunset lay within 't,
And thou hast touched anew
Into softness every tint.

If ever thou didst fling
Omens from the bird's grey wing,
(As certain these as Oscines,)
If there be a lover dying,
And he sigh upon his knees,
Bring him comfort in his sighing.

If ever thou didst scance
In a wayward wistful dance
Up and down like a frown,
On the wall with giant scrawl,
Till the soul would sink and drown
In the waste and glimmering wall:

If ever thou didst stand
In a staircase stark and grand,
And on that spot in ghastly knot
Didst seem to stir and squeak ;
Affright that lover not,
If he with death be weak.

For if his love should weep
In some violet-lidded sleep,
The tears arise in her sweet eyes
Like a golden shadow-fit ;
And her blush it flits and flies
As the shadows fly and flit.

And what is likest thee ?
What makes thee dear to me ?
The blush and tremble which fain dissemble
How much of mine is hers ;
The very blush and tremble
Which her sweet pride demurs.

Ode to Joy.

Too long hast thou been lost; the cup has left
  My pallid lips; too bitter overlong
The draught had grown ; a hideous poison eft
  Swam upwards towards the quaffing mouth, a wrong
Was done by nature's nectar to my youth;
  So with us all; a pallid spectral troop,
Whose thoughts are grey ere age be come in sooth,
  We sit together, and together stoop,
Hiding with hands our faces, when the cloud
  Of memory from the deep with thunderous rain
Swells up against us; then, ah, then we shroud
  Our faces from the iron-driving pain,
In horror bowed.

A ghostly company, be sure, are we;
  At thought of joy our eyes are full of tears;
We cannot walk with lovers on the lea,
  We dare not have sweet music in our ears;

We toiled through spring for summer's golden sheaf,
    And for our harvest found we hemlock strewn;
Ah, why, when we were cursed beyond belief,
    For other hearts should Fortune keep her boon ?
Not so, believe us, sorrow is the lot
    Of all who look for joy beneath the moon;
Come, pace the shore that leads thee to our grot,
    While o'er blue waters dies the bygone tune,
Rejoicing not.

Behold the white clouds roll along the blue,
    And like the clouds do flocks o'erspread the plain;
And like them winds the forest out of view;
    Shall not Joy's chariot come with splendid train,
And he descend and walk the living air,
    With Melody and Peace, and Happy Love,
Wing-footed, rosy-limbed, with myrtle rare
    And olive crowned from old Eleusis' grove ?
Ah, no, the fury night will soon be here;
    She comes with storms that drive the flocks away,
And takes the large free clouds to make her bier,
    And rends the leaves ; no longer youth can stay
Nor joy appear.

The Vision of Thebes.

TRUE poesy is thought impassionëd,
Moulded of form, sound, colour ; and so wed
To outer life : she is the pure ideal
Transferred to use, refiner of the real :
She sleeps unstirred till won from intellect
By passion, the great mover, and so deck'd
In many coloured life : nor loses she
Aught of her secret grace and purity
By such strong contact with this outwardness,
Else were she formless, voiceless, imageless,
A slumbrous phantom, brighter, subtiler
Than sunshine upon wide-spun gossamer,
But void and mute, an unfulfilled decree,
An aimless power, a realmless deity.
Yet now she lives insphcred within the world,
Haunting all time with music, and empearled
In all the preciousness of outer life,
The child of beauty, sprung from gentle strife
Of influences diverse, yet supreme,
Whereby the soul is joined with heaven's scheme.

Therefore the past is glorious; and each place
Wherein the past has been, wherein the race
Of man hath moved is holy; 'tis the lair
Of passions yet unspent ; therein they swear
That oft the wind hath utterance not its own,
Pregnant with airy meaning; there have flown
Shapes half-seen by their shadows, which but glance,
Then mock the sudden eye; there oft the dance
Of phantasy is pressed upon the dew ;
There whispery fens have music, often too
From barren, ruined, wasteful solitudes
Great sounds have sprung, swollen on the swell of woods,
And mingled with night gushings of far streams,
Floated and died; these were the first stray gleams
Of the great dawn of legend, and in sooth
It might be so, for legend oft spheres truth,
And the great cycle ever hath onrolled,
Changeful of form, but certain to unfold
Weird broideries of time ; like as the years
Glide in quaternion, still the harbingers
Of life and beauty, though in each the dower
Differs in depth of season, sun, or shower.
    Thus then her chiefest glory earth has won
From man's reflected presence, as the sun
Flushes with purple heaven's wide westering side,
And that again the sea : I oft have tried
In sorry sort to image to my sense
Fair cities, and the bygone opulence

Of ruined wastes; and, certes, howsoe'er
Legends be true, yet oft to poet there,
Where most the shadows of time's wings have gloomed,
Have come sweet dreams, which almost have assumed
Bodily shapes, the concourse of swift thought,
Which but for very transience would be nought.
Such me befel, a vision of past gladness,
Filled with the rayless imagery of sadness,
Big with the glories, darkened with the woe
Of nations dead, and ages long ago.
And I must try a strange and antique theme,
The dim remembrance of a flitted dream;
And I must venture on far wanderings,
Dimming my soul in underlights of things.
      I had a vision, and the past came to me;
She touched me with her voice—her voice ran through
      me:
She was a shadow, that strange phantasy,
A trembler upon being, moving wearily;
Her voice an echo, shadow's utterance,
A shadow and an echo ! then a trance
Fell on my senses, but my spirit sped,
A mystic pinion, wheresoe'er she led.
Then came I to an awful place, afar,
Upon the midmost tide of night, and there
I saw a stony whiteness answering
Unto the moon's uncertain glimmering :
There were dim forms of tower and pyramid
Narrowing skywards, but all else was hid,

By the false breadths of the uncertain light:
Midway a river rolled through the deep night,
Black, weltering sullenly; and lo, thereon,
Cinctured with imaged beams the image of the moon.
Then entered I the place with secret dread,
Passing through streets of ruin, where my tread
Fell drearily, for it was very lone,
And full of wasteful haunts, and far agone
In desolation: columns stood there shorn
Of half their height, and massy fragments torn
From fallen piles, and crumbling, fissured walls,
And sunken towers and domes, and capitals
Broken on bases: there too images
Of nameless shapes, supporting cornices,
Stood in half-lights: and to the chill night air
A few scant trees sighed sadly: everywhere
Shadows fell black on shadows, but all round
The outermost, unbroken, reached the ground.
Much marvelling at this so grievous change
Upon such grandeur wrought, and giving range
To many fancies, till the stars were sped
Far into morn, in that untenanted
And voiceless place throughout the night I stood,
But when the dawn betrayed the secret quietude,
Then saw I clearly all the mystery
Of obelisk and tower, all emblemry
Of cornice-couchant sphinx with calm wide eyes,
All wonders of dim-reaching galleries,

Of crumbling frieze, of ruining gradine,
Of marbled slab, of moulding palatine ;
Moreover when the clearness of daylight
Slid into distant haze, there seemed upright,
Fronting the east, a giant mass of stone,
Shaped into man's rough semblance, whereupon
Unto my brain swift recognition ran :
Memnon I knew, and Thebes Egyptian.
　　Ay, 'twas the glorious city, hundred-gated,
The olden one, before which stand abated
All puny elegance of modern days,
Whose cumbrous grandeur even to our gaze
Fills out all myths of founder demigod;
The stony ghost of old, the sea-bank broad,
Staying time's waves, which, with its great compeers,
Stands forth unwhelmed by the huge tide of years ;
Gazing whereon we may uptrace the springs
Of human action through the past of things,
And scoop the future from the past—such thought
Rose in my heart, with fear and wonder fraught,
Unshaped in word, till from my breast unpent
My voice at length throughout the ruins went.
　　All without grief, 'twas thus I cried aloud,
Is light and flitting as a rainless cloud ;
And thou, fair city, hast a name, and fate
Dewing all time with tears, for thou dost mate
Thyself unto an inner region
Of glory and decay.　Ah, once the throne

Whereon erewhile towered brave humanity
Enseated grandly, dost thou prostrate lie?
Alas, not ruined shade of portico
Nor fall of turret strength hath brought thee low
To this immortal mourning; thou dost show
The truth outrolled by rolling centuries
Of glorious but changing destinies.
The heart of man is one ! throughout all life
At grasp with circumstance, at endless strife
To clothe itself in deed ; but as no brain
Hath e'er been found capacious to contain
An ultimate ideal, accident
Entails itself on all that we invent,
Nor aught is perfect, nothing can attain
Its final point at once, but still must gain
By slow accessions, still must be increased
By added strength; hence nought hath ever ceased,
All life is reproduction; hence upspring
Cities, with all their wealthy minist'ring
To diverse wants, which ever couchant lie
In different natures; hence society
Is holden in the bond of difference
And hence compacted; hence, great Thebes, hence,
The impulse that created thee still moves
Unslumbrous and unspent, for what man loves
Is ever changeless, and becomes the centre
Whence he draws wider circles; do thou enter

11

Among those wondrous antitypes of soul
Which show it like yet diverse, be the goal
At once, and starting-point of human thought !

Ah ! subtle cause thine overthrow hath wrought,
Who whilom sat'st the crown of circumstance,
Taking joy's tithe from every moment, glance
Upon thyself, and say, are not the powers
Of ruin sown within ?   Thy sister towers
Stand on in their first strength, by battle's wrack
Unbroken, by time's ever ruthless track
Scarce furrowed ; what then was it that hath cast
Earth's darkness on thee, making thee at last
A sepulchre for ruin ?   Sad, that e'er
Man's glory should be made his sepulchre !
Yea, that one idea driven to excess
Should be its own destroyer !   Thou didst press
Thy law of sole dominion questionless
Unto its furthest; thou didst give no scope
To individual purpose, interest, hope,
Those parents of endeavour ; and the want
Of this one truth it was did disenchant
Thy solemn halls ; thy stern unswerving code
On alien ages sunk its unmeet load,
Nor knew to fit itself to after years.
So to its rules old tyranny adheres,
The season being gone, in fell despite
Of change and progress, and forgetting quite

That man's advancing work can never die,
And all must share the immortality.

Thus mused I till the richness of the west,
Of hues immingled in a floating rest,
Showed like a melted rainbow, till adown
Fluttering in thousand stars great night had flown.
I mused; I saw the budding moon enshrined
By gentlest office of the summer wind,
With clouds to couch on; and in that still hour
Great visions stood enshapèd by the power
That works in earnest meditation: lo!
Methought the place so gloom-entranced ere now
Had met the noonlight, and a dream in dream
Fell on my soul, for all the air did seem
Enthronged with uplift shapes of tower and fane,   \
Each bearing strange device upon its van
Of hieroglyph; and 'neath them life again
Was multiplied in dusky throngs of men,
And from collision groups of circumstance
Sprang ever chequered; 'twas as though advance
Of onward-flowing time had never been
Since first that desert was joy's chosen scene.
For ruin was not: the great city's smoke
Swung heavy in the sky, and voices spoke
In the wide-whispering night, borne from beneath
To the upper air, far wafted on the breath
Of grief or laughter: midst a mighty throng
I entered, borne resistlessly along

11—2

By the great human concourse, through long streets
Walled by vast columns and enset with sheets
Of pale red marble; ever as I went
The wonder grew, for all the crowd upsent
Red pointed flames of torchlight to the sky,
As on they marched beneath emblazonry
Hung high from palace roof or pillar tall,
As suited ancient Thebes upon a festival.

    There were vast forms of calm eternal lines,
That brooded ever upon guarded shrines;
There were slight nameless creatures with scythed wings,
Embodied thoughts and delicatest things
In fretwork, whereon ever flitted past
Warm hurried glows and moving shadows cast
From torches, and made thinner by the moon;
Unto a temple huge the crowd rolled on,
And passed between its valves of crudded gold,
Into a four-square court wide to enfold
The vastest throng that e'er to worship passed,
Round which went curtains always interlaced,
From shaft to shaft wide floating; and entraced
With tender curves of richest broidery,
That showed upon the clear and moony sky.
O'erhead the fane loomed hugely, and in front
Two doors of inwrought glory nigh a font
O'erdrooped by heavy-leavèd orient trees,
Drew all eyes towards them; for the mysteries
Of Egypt's greatest god were shrinèd there.

Now when the joyous torches sunken were,
And the glad shoutings hushed for reverence,
And one sole voice was telling how immense
The glory and the terror and the wrath,
And prayer was breathing thoughts unuttered forth,
Back I withdrew me from the golden glare,
Back from the awèd throng, apart to where
Was only moonlight in a quiet street.
And there the far-off echoes did I meet
Of the full-throated response, and stray gleams
Of magic lights, and heard the voice of streams.
The broad-breast river ran through floating shades,
Lapping sheer blocks of granite, colonnades
That high upheld long rows of palaces ;
And on its eddies glanced light pinnaces
With lamps and wafts of music : on I hied,
Methought in silence, lone and unespied,
Beneath vast groves of sleeping foliage,
The stars among their branches; soft umbrage
Moon-flung on sheeny fountains, where there lay
Enwalled spaces widened to embay
Quaint plots of greenness : then with sudden change
Methought I was amid an endless range
Of palace fronts, tall shafts, and long arcades,
And slabbed steps that led through balustrades
Of columns twin on either hand, which spread
Into an archèd roof high overhead

Through all the aislèd length ; each floor was paven
With level squares of marble, gem-engraven,
Which chilled the moonbeams streaming over them ;
And on the doors was wealth of gold and gem,
A solemn wealth, which gave to the moonlight
Rich molten gleams ; and fountain rillets bright,
Jetted from marble stems by water elves,
Came spreaded over smooth and level shelves,
Wave rippling over wave ; and thence they fell
With ceaseless murmur and a gentle swell
Unto the marble limits of their lake.
Thus momently did I myself betake
Through golden vestibules and galleries
Into wide palace courts and breadth of terraces :
Till in the midst of this wide loveliness
Close sandalled forms about me 'gan to press,
And I was in amongst the throng again :
And that great heart, whence through the whole domain
Of Egypt, life was pulsed, throbbed mightily,
In its primeval strength before mine eye.
    But now these visions warm began to pale,   '
Gradual as fogbank parting from a vale ;
The night was sinking, and the stars were dim,
And soon the morning light began to swim
Slow through the eastern port with saddening gleam ;
A hundred fountains twisted the first beam
In crystal writhings, then all straight were gone,
And all the show, and I was left alone.

Babylon and Nineveh.

From desert land the Arab sheikh is come across the
    southern sea;
And now his camel skirts the wastes that lead him
    through the old Chaldee;
He watches not the gannet flying over towards the
    setting sun,
But marks the bittern and its shadow on the pools of
    Babylon.

'Twas written in the Burden her destruction should as
    sudden be
As Sodom and Gomorrah sunk beneath the waters of
    the sea;
And still they say that often he who sails upon those
    languid waves,
At ebb sees whitely gleaming palaces and spires in
    ocean caves,

As underneath the ocean are preserved the Cities of the
  Plain,
So by the fire preserved to us, the towers of Bel and
  Nin remain;
No earthquake could have kept them as the fire that
  wrought their overthrow;
And every age has deeper sealed that mortal sleep so
  soft and low.

And rivers that run swiftly thither from the mountains
  of their birth,
Go ever from them slowly, big with slime, and dust,
  and fire-baked earth:
Then all their ancient limits on their heedless way they
  overpass,
Until at last the plain is swamped beneath the festering
  morass.

Ah! once their cry was in their ships; the old Phœnician
  galleys went
From thence; and Tyre and Sidon were Chaldea's
  mighty monument:
Ponders the lonely sheikh, as o'er the waste the
  swinging camel speeds;
The Kufa far behind him with its steersman dark and
  gaunt recedes.

Then here is Babylon: behold the fiery cloud of the
   simoon
Hangs o'er its shapeless mounds in vaporous setting of
   the afternoon;
So o'er a lonely gravestone might a widow's dusky
   garments sweep,
As that wild wanderer surveys it from Borsippa's
   crumbled steep.

Beneath those quiet heaps how many dead are sleeping;
    there they lie,
The old Chaldean glory, all the pomp and all the
   imag'ry;
The temples and the palaces, the hanging gardens and
   the walls,
The friezes upon pavements strewn, the bases upon
   capitals.

Still rises here the Kasr, Nebúchadnezzar reared in
   days fifteen,
And fronting it in solemn state the huger Babil mound
   is seen ;
And once upon that very place where now he stands
   upon the Tel,
Stood bearded kings and sages, and the votive offerings
   smoked to Bel.

To the seven planets rose that temple with its chord of
  colours bright;
To form the planetary spheres the sacred band of hues
  unite;
Black, orange, red, gold, yellow, blue, the silver symbol
  of the moon,
And so sprang the storeys in a mystic harmony of tune.

From mound to mound the grass is spread, by ruin
  raised in swathes of green;
It leads the eye from height to height o'er all the mute
  and desert scene;
And here are recent traces where some roving Arab
  camp was laid :
It was the caravan that here one little stage its journey
  stayed.

Do not these vestiges of man unseal the giant grave
  beneath?
The latest trace of human life interpret best the ancient
  death?
More ghastly are the cinders of the latest fire that here
  was lit,
Than mound of ruin sleeping calmly with the smoulder-
  ing cloud on it.

And 'twixt this generation and the last a distance
intervenes,
More vast than lies between the many centuries the ruin
screens :
Than lies between the king the Persian army slew, and
Naram-sin,—
The king who ruled primevally before the sceptre
passed to Nin.

In ruin all confounded lie; and Erech is their tranquil
tomb ;
Lo ! far on the horizon looms the Babylonian catacomb ;
There coffins, piled in mountains, of their ancient sleep
are dispossessed
By hordes of shuddering Moslems and the busy searchers
of the West.

They yield them from their cedar shelves and crumble
from their stony bier ;
They sink upon the alien decks ; on river drifts they
disappear ;
And gain far off a foreign home, by stranger eyes and
hands defiled ;
From this depopulated land the very dead shall be
exiled.

To north, behold, another river pours its life-blood to
the sea ;
Behold another city-circle girding ancient Nineveh ;
Most ancient Asshur, holy Calah, Arbil, Khazah, Khor-
sabad ;
Half were capitals, ere Nineveh herself the chief
dominion had.

And now they lie around her, now the sorrow of the
earth on all ;
Strange silence that hath long endured, and coldness in
the charnel hall ;
What man dare sit within it, as the tunnelled light is
stealing round
On sculptured slabs of pallid stone, that form the walls,
and strew the ground ?

The fire-bleached gypsum shines again, the awful
bearded kings are viewed
Amid the courts where once they wrote their deeds in
living attitude ;
'Tis they who taught the sword to range in ways before
unknown to man
From Zagros to the Western Sea, from Egypt to the
Caspian.

On swords this first of empires rose, and not as bringing
    peace by war
They ruled o'er prostrate nations, but as warrior o'er
    warrior;
Each king his standard drew along the scene of his
    forefathers' toils,
As rends the griffin o'er and o'er the dragon's still
    rebelling coils.

Each king in god-like battle joy upon his warring
    chariot stands,
Scourging the prostrate foe with rain of bitter arrows
    from his hands :
They scale the walls of mighty forts, the rivers deep
    and wide they ford;
They cut their way through pathless woods, they build
    their city with the sword.

The eagle rides upon their rein ; the winged circle with
    them speeds,
That living wheel prophetic, prescient, nimbus of eternal
    deeds ;
And here behold the votive bulls, in mystic legend
    gravely wrought,
Ox-limbed for strength, gier-winged for speed, and
    fronted like a man for thought.

Ah! now they fade at once, in sudden waning of the
    Eastern light,
By grave and mound their multitudes are swallowed
    up in kindly night;
And whether night of hours or ages, matters not at all
    to Pul;
Yet that poor Arab waits for daylight in his lodging at
    Mosul.

THE END.

LONDON:

PRINTED BY SMITH, ELDER AND CO.,

LITTLE GREEN ARBOUR COURT, OLD BAILEY, E.C.